RESCUED BY THE MOUNTAIN MAN

DANA ALDEN

Amanda Hildreth jumped at the chance to start life anew in the booming town of Virginia City in Montana Territory. She heads West to work at her stepbrother's mercantile and maybe find love one day. But, her mule train is attacked before she even gets there.

Mountain Man Cal Ayers agrees to lead Amanda safely across the mountains. It's not long, though, before they realize the attack was aimed at Amanda – and that living with her stepbrother might not be the safest plan.

Amanda can't establish a new life when someone is trying to kill her. And she can't imagine a new life without Cal, who she's falling for. But Cal is fighting his feelings as he is already engaged. Can Cal save Amanda's life, and their burgeoning love, in time?

Dedicated to my husband, Chuck
"Everything To Me"

CHAPTER 1

AUGUST 1865

Amanda hurried toward the large spruce trees and the downed branches and bushes surrounding them at the edge of the forest. She glanced back over her shoulder. She could still see the men in camp, but they were not paying her any mind. They were packing up, though, and would soon notice her absence. She turned back and quickly climbed over a log, pulling her long skirts free from the catching brush.

Two months on the road had led her farther and farther from civilization. She'd ventured from the cobbled streets of Lowell, Massachusetts, rumbling with the sounds of the many mills churning out goods and smoke, across the whole country, to this: Montana Territory. From her women's boarding house with its two decent meals a day, a chamber pot, and a lovely settee in the parlor, to this: hiding in the bushes to do her business. What she wouldn't do for an outhouse.

On the plains, when the wagon train had still contained families and women, and, indeed, actual wagons, she'd had the privacy of a chamber pot inside the wagon. It hadn't been terribly private, what with Geraldine on her sick bed inside, but it had been safe. Now, Amanda was the only woman member of a pack mule train, and though she could find privacy in the trees of the mountain foothills, she couldn't help but think of the stories she'd heard about the many wild animals roaming there.

Amanda chose a secluded spot behind the tree. She hitched her skirts up around her knees and squatted to do her business. She chose a leaf that she hoped would not cause her skin to rash.

Finished, she shook out her skirt and scurried back to the camp. Ahead she could see the pack mules were loaded and the riding horses almost so.

"Nearly time, Miss Amanda," said Mr. Smith, the pack master. He was an older man, probably forty-five years in her estimation, with wiry arms and a long scraggly beard, half gray. Smith had not seen his own daughter in many years, and Amanda thought that was why the pack master had allowed a lone woman to join the group.

She saw that he had taken her packed bag and already loaded it, along with the breakfast box of pans and dishes. She was grateful to him for taking her on, giving her a horse to ride in exchange for cooking and mending on the journey. Grateful, because she'd needed to leave the wagon train she had been on but didn't have the money or supplies to travel on her own. So, she'd tried to earn her place.

"Look there, Smitty," called Scamp, the young man who worked with Mr. Smith crossing back and forth from Fort Laramie in Nebraska Territory to Virginia City in Montana Territory. They led would-be miners and all sorts of supplies in and took the failed miners—and occasionally a successful one —back to civilization and on to spend their fortunes back East.

Amanda looked up to see Scamp, all angles and elbows,

pointing past her in the direction from which she had just come. She looked over her shoulder to see a genuine Mountain Man—just as described in the penny dreadfuls she'd read—walking toward them… from the copse of trees where she had been just moments before.

He wore a chambray shirt under a coat of tanned skins. His leather breeches were worn to a dull shine in many places. He had brown hair pulled back in a queue, brown brows, a short, scruffy beard, and weather-tanned skin with creases at his eyes. His arm was raised in greeting to the calls from Mr. Smith and Scamp, showing off the leather fringe decorating his sleeve. He wore a possibles bag off his shoulder and a rifle that looked like something Amanda's grandfather had used.

His erect bearing and long stride indicated a strong man.

Amanda felt the heat rush to her cheeks. He couldn't have seen her—could he? No, she was sure she'd have seen him. She had looked for men in the direction of camp and wild animals in the other and would surely have seen a man nearby.

He walked toward Mr. Smith and seemed not to notice Amanda. *Oh, please*, she thought. And then, at the last moment, he looked at her and one corner of his mouth crooked in a hint of a smile. His eyes—blue—told her what she'd feared. Yes, he had seen her and he was laughing at her. How mortifying!

EVEN AS CAL SHOOK HANDS WITH SMITTY, HE COULD FEEL the heat washing off the face of the pretty young woman. She looked fit to be tied. He'd only caught a glimpse of her in the woods and turned away, but clearly, she imagined a peeping Tom following her every move. Years in the wilderness had taught him to walk as silently as he could, and he'd become even more cautious when he heard rustling ahead of him.

He wondered why she hadn't had her husband or father, or whoever she was traveling with, keep an eye out for her.

"Good to see you, Smitty," he said. "Scamp." Cal greeted the boy, perhaps fifteen now, with a handshake and saw his narrow shoulders pull back when he realized he was being greeted as a man.

"I was up there," he gestured up to an overlook on the mountain, "and saw your pack line last evening. I'm surprised you made it through with such a small group though. But glad." He only saw Smitty, Scamp, the pretty woman, and three other men. No wagons to circle, no one who looked particularly strong with guns. "Maybe you haven't heard all the news."

Smitty glanced at Scamp and the girl and nodded. Cal could tell he understood the message: *I saw you, and others did and will, too.* It was risky enough following John Bozeman's new trail, but with the attacks between the whites and the Blackfoot Indians up by Fort Benton, relations with the Indians were particularly difficult.

"See anything else up there? Crow? Blackfoot?" Smitty asked as he checked the ropes tying his pack mules in a line. Cal knew the ropes were always tied right, but that's why Smitty was good at what he did.

"No, though I ran across some white men a couple of days ago that seemed out of place."

Smitty nodded and said nothing. There were problems with Indians who didn't like the influx of whites that came along with the discovery of gold. And groups like this, ones that crossed Indian Territory to shorten their long journey, were taking an extra risk. But there was an equal, if usually not quite so deadly, problem with whites who gave up their dreams of mining their fortunes in Bannack or Virginia City and turned to thievery instead. These were the ones who'd come West to make their fortune, but not to earn it.

"What brings you out this way?"

"I was checking for signs of animals, seeing where I'd lay traps this winter. I thought I might come east a little farther than usual and find you on your way in. Some news you might like to hear." Cal smiled. "And even a mountain man needs a little human company occasionally."

At that, he turned to the hovering Scamp, grabbed him in his arms, and began an awkward dance that caused a rush of red across the boy's face and a loud laugh from Smitty.

The pretty gal, on the other hand, was viewing him with a scrunched-up nose. She didn't seem to approve of dancing in the warm morning sun.

"So, what kind of news are you bringing?" asked Smitty.

Cal stopped spinning but kept his arm around Scamp's shoulders, amused as the kid tried to tug away. Strong and wiry, he was, but not as strong as Cal. "Some action up by Fort Benton. A new Territorial Secretary—an Irishman. That kind of news."

Smitty nodded. "Where's your horse? You can ride with us and fill me in." Smitty turned to the pretty girl, also hovering nearby. Cal thought she was hoping stillness would make him forget she was there.

"Miss Amanda Hildreth, this here is Calvin Ayers. Let Cal help you up on Pony. Scamp, check Cotton's pack there. You still haven't got the hang of balancing the weight. Everyone," his voice rose, "mount up!" Scamp spun himself out of Cal's arm with a grin and high-tailed it over to the mule.

Cal nodded. Smitty knew him well enough to know his horse and mule were tied up behind the trees. He didn't like to draw attention to his animals or what they packed. He turned to Amanda. She looked him in the eye and blushed anew.

"Smitty is letting you ride Pony? He must have a soft spot for you."

"He isn't 'letting' me ride Pony," she said, squaring her shoulders. "I'm earning my way and Pony is part of the deal."

Cal was tempted to tease her and see if her face could get any redder.

He raised his eyebrows to her and she gasped.

"Cooking! Mending!" she hissed.

Smitty had mounted up and started hawing his mules.

"No time to waste," said Cal. He grabbed her about the waist and lifted her onto the small pinto horse. The black and white of the horse contrasted with the blond of the girl and made her stand out more than she already did, which was quite a bit in his mind. He put the reins into her hands, grabbed her feet and put them in the stirrups, and smacked the horse on the rear. Pony began walking alongside the pack mules.

Cal turned to find himself face to face with a thin man in a cleric's collar. The man's voice was trailing off, "I will help…" but it was clearly too late. Cal could tell by the man's alarmed eyes that a mountain man was both scary and worthy of disdain. Not worthy, at least, to touch the pretty blond Amanda. Cal looked him up and down.

The man was decent but heading toward threadbare, appropriate for a small mid-west town, but not a long hard ride over the plains and mountains. His hair was a greasy yellow and Cal suspected the Yellowstone River had been too cold for this man to bathe in. He laughed to himself…it didn't get much warmer than it was now, but it got a whole lot colder.

Amanda was riding off and the two men were staring at each other. It felt like a pissing contest, but Cal could see Amanda wasn't paying this man any attention, and he himself had only just been introduced, so why this man was threatened by Cal… it was absurd. Admittedly, there were few white women in the area, and virtually none unencumbered by a husband or father, which this gal seemed to be.

And she was young and handsome, too.

Having been alone in the forest for weeks, Cal knew how to be quiet. He simply stood and looked. The man shifted, looked away and back, shifted again. He had something to say, it seemed. Cal waited, and finally said, "You're going to miss your train." Though the last horse in line was a mere ten paces away, the man jumped with widened eyes. He turned to his horse, turned back to Cal, gave him his second glare of the morning, and scurried to his bow-legged steed and heaved himself up.

With a *hmmmpf*, he and his horse followed on the line. Horses were herd animals and wouldn't want to be left behind, but clearly, the skinny pastor didn't know it.

Cal strode back toward the trees. He'd gather his horse and mule and cut across the hill, catching up with Smitty's group directly. As he walked through the golden grass, he caught a glimpse of a bright shine out the corner of his eye, a reflection of the sun off a gun barrel in the distance.

CHAPTER 2

"**M**iss Amanda! Miss Amanda!"

Ugh, she thought. Pastor Frank was bumping along on his horse in her direction. They were all headed the same way so it would be directly toward her anyway, but she knew he was headed to her specifically. The young pastor—really, he was probably a couple of years older than her but seemed as young and annoying as some of the boys she'd grown up with—had made it his mission to save her. She wondered why he didn't focus on Scamp, clearly growing up without the Lord... or on Richard and Dick, the twin brothers on their way to mine their fortune if they didn't drink themselves to death first. Of course, with parents who named them such, it wasn't a wonder they weren't too swift themselves.

"Miss Amanda!" Pastor Frank blew out with a breath. He seemed to get out of breath just riding slowly, which was a trick, Amanda thought. "Are you alright?"

"Should I not be?"

"I'm so sorry I wasn't in time to stop that mountain man from accosting you." He looked so concerned, so contrite.

9

She'd been mortified, knowing Mr. Ayers had seen her in the trees, but the man had actually not done anything beyond express amusement at her expense. Perhaps more importantly, she disliked the pastor's claim of protector. He had introduced her to Mr. Smith and thus enabled her to change plans after Geraldine died and Amanda's situation had become unbearable, but she didn't need him guarding her from a mere lift onto a horse. She had taken care of herself in Lowell, and she could do so here… mostly.

Perhaps even more importantly, she saw that Mr. Smith liked and respected this man, despite her own impression, and that said a lot. He certainly didn't have time for the likes of Pastor Frank. In fact, Frank had tried to follow her into the trees once, "for protection." He had talked over her dismissal, citing bears as a danger and patting the gun that he carried so awkwardly. Finally, Smitty had barked at him.

"Bears don't want to meet you any more than you want to meet them. She makes a little noise and she's fine. Leave the girl to her privacy."

"She'll be dead before she'll realize you were wrong," said Pastor Frank. "There are bears everywhere!"

"You've seen some bear scat and now you're the expert, eh?" Luckily, a distraction arose. "Is that your horse wandering off, Pastor? Do I need to show you a proper knot again?" Frank had run off while Smitty rolled his eyes, grumbling how he'd have been better off if the preacher had gone to that other Virginia City in Nevada; Amanda had run off into the trees grateful of the privacy.

Pastor Frank continued speaking. "I don't want to be offensive, but these mountain men live in the woods alone—without a woman—for months at a time. The first one they see… is in danger. I don't know how else to say that to you."

Amanda knew what he meant. As one of the few women traveling to Montana Territory alone, she'd encountered her share of male attention. It was why she found herself out there, instead of on the southerly wagon route as originally intended. But, she couldn't feel at risk in this particular camp of men that had so far looked out for her. Nor had she felt a sense of danger from that mountain man, Calvin Ayers.

"Please, Pastor Frank, you mustn't imagine I was in danger being assisted onto a horse. I am fine." She tapped her heels to Pony's sides to encourage a brisker pace. No matter, the pastor and his bowlegged horse followed.

She tried again. "Really, I am aware of the dangers and will be prepared when necessary. Smitty—I mean, Mr. Smith—knows his business and I am confident in his protection of our train."

Frank didn't like her attempts to get away. "Really, and when you get to Virginia City? What then?"

"I will find my brother."

"Miss Amanda. What if your step-brother doesn't welcome you, or can't?"

She'd made the mistake of revealing to the pastor that she'd left for her new life without either invitation or even acknowledgement from her stepbrother. It had been at Fort Laramie when the pastor had been solicited to say the service for Geraldine and her stillborn twins. He'd been awkward and hesitating, explaining it was his first funeral. But he hadn't been at all hesitant when she revealed she wanted to leave the wagon train, and the service of Geraldine's now-widowed husband. Pastor Frank had led her straight to Mr. Smith, and his shepherding had increased from there.

"I will find the Female Boarding House and I will find work."

Frank choked. He fumbled to find words and clasped his hands tightly. "I don't think you're that kind of woman," he said.

So many men were against women working or living away

from their families. In Lowell, where so many women worked in the mills, it wasn't so shocking, but even there…

"I will." *I have done so already*, she thought.

"You wouldn't," he said with his hands still clasped together, though it was hard to say whether in frustration or prayer.

"Yes," said Amanda proudly. "I would. I will do what it takes to make my fortune and my new life out West."

The horses ambled along. The clop of the many hooves, the twitter of a few birds, the rustling of leaves and grass were the only sounds.

"Please," said Frank, "I think you're better than that. I am sure of it." He took a deep breath. "Be my wife. I will support you, and you will support our family and my ministry." Amanda was stunned. Her horse stumbled and she took her time regaining her grip on the reins. How could she respond to him, one who clearly meant well, even if she felt he was misguided?

And then he spoke more.

"You are too gentle and God-fearing a woman. You don't belong in a Boarding House. You belong with your family of birth, and then your family of marriage. Your father, and then your husband, will care for you. Do not turn from God."

Turn from God? All because she chose to leave home for the mills, to make money she could send home to her family after her father's accident? Because she chose to come out West when he'd recovered and no longer needed the money, and when the mills had exacted their toll? This man did not know her—and nor would he! Not with that pompous attitude.

"Do not judge me! There's nothing wrong with hard labor." Amanda was exasperated.

"I wish," Pastor Frank offered in a surprising turn, "I wish I had more experience in counseling my flock. I wish I could help you better."

Amanda didn't know how to reply to that. She could tell he meant well, but in her aggravation, it was hard to be charitable. She took her own deep breath. "You can pray for me," she said. "I'm sure you are practiced at prayer."

The Pastor's face lit up, and he looked younger and lighter of heart than he had in days. Amanda had to remind herself that this journey was difficult and scary for everyone.

☙❧

After Pastor Frank allowed his horse to fall behind, Amanda felt free to turn her attention to the landscape. They followed the Yellowstone River toward a huge mountain range —the Rockies. The river meandered in a valley between two flat-topped hills. *Buttes* they were called.

To the north was a single large mountain, all alone.

It reminded her of a print she had seen in a gallery last year on her Sunday afternoon off—Mount Fuji in the country of Japan. The sky was clear of clouds and bright in color—*a bluebird day* according to Mr. Smith. She saw three big-eared deer—mule deer she'd been told—grazing in the distance. When startled, they ran in a hopping, up-down fashion that amused her.

That thought of amusement led her to think again of Calvin Ayers. She hadn't liked how he'd been amused at her expense. She wondered how he ended up a mountain man… if his inappropriate social behavior was because he lived alone in the woods or was it why he'd ended up alone in the woods in the first place?

She smiled, contemplating.

Mr. Ayers was a fairly young man, not old and grizzled like the ones she'd heard about. Were there mountain women, too? Families that raised mountain men?

These were silly thoughts; he'd been sociable with Mr.

Smith and Scamp, and helpful to her. He'd also been gentle-manly enough not mention what he'd seen of her... she felt her cheeks heating up again.

She saw a movement in the distance and saw emerging from the woods a man riding a horse and leading a big mule. It was that Calvin Ayers, she realized. He leaned low on his horse's neck, urging it on with his legs. The pack mule followed along at the end of its lead, its heavy packs heaving under the ropes. They moved at a fair clip at a diagonal that would join their pack train up at the next bend in the river. This was too fast for a social call; clearly, something was wrong.

Amanda touched her heels to Pony's sides and sped up.

CHAPTER 3

Amanda tapped her heels to Pony's sides and trotted up the line to Mr. Smith, who had paused to await Mr. Ayers. He was scanning around them, looking in every direction.

"Mr. Smith?" she asked.

"Hold tight, Miss Amanda," he said, barely glancing at her.

Mr. Ayers rode up next to them. He briefly met Amanda's eyes but if there was a message in it, she couldn't read it. He turned to Smith. "You're being stalked, from at least two different places." He tilted his head toward one copse of trees and then toward a rocky butte.

"Here's what we're going to do," said Ayers. "I'll turn up toward Crazy Mountain. I'll loosen my mule's rope so she breaks loose before we hit the culvert. If they're looking for easy pickings they'll go for her and her pack and leave us alone."

Smitty nodded, his jaw tight and lips pinched. He didn't look terribly optimistic.

"And if they don't?" Amanda asked.

The two men met eyes. Mr. Ayers answered. "I'll circle around behind them. I'm a good shot and they're likely not interested in dying."

The clear blue sky and bright sun that had seemed so lovely moments before now made Amanda feel hot and exposed.

The pack train continued walking briskly along the trail. The mules and horses had their heads up. Ears twitched and eyes rolled. They sensed something, too. Pastor Frank hovered next to Amanda. Scamp, Richard and Dick hugged the mule train, hands resting on guns and powder bags, eyes sharp.

Pastor Frank leaned over his saddle pommel toward Mr. Ayers and Smitty. "If that would work, why not dump all the packs and make a run for it?"

Smitty answered in a hard low voice. "First of all, people paid for and are depending on those supplies, up ahead. Second of all, you may be on a one-way trip, but packing is my livelihood. If I start dumping my packs I might as well give up and just gift-wrap 'em next time. The desperados will be lined up waiting to claim my goods – and likely a mule or two to help haul it away."

Pastor Frank tucked his chin into his collar, eyes downcast, and gave a small nod to Smitty.

"Will they follow so obvious a diversion then, Mr. Ayers, if you let loose your mule?" Amanda asked. She held one hand on the reins and the other on the pommel. The rocky terrain and quick pace caused Pony to rock and stumble and she feared her distraction would allow her to fall. She glanced up to see the mountain man eyeing her with a hint of impatience.

"I'll try to make it look less than obvious. An accident when I'm hauling out to protect myself." His eyes left her face so he could keep surveying their surroundings, intense and serious. "And once we're safe, I'll hunt them down and reclaim my animal and property."

Cal's deadly serious tone sent a shiver up Amanda's spine. She nodded, not knowing how else to respond to him.

"Hang on tight, Miss Amanda," said Smitty. "Scamp, you keep those mules a-movin'. When we reach that outcropping up there, we can hunker down."

Apparently, the followers knew that, too, and the plan was thwarted. Shots rang out. Even as dirt exploded and rock shards flew, the group as one sped toward the rocks. Ayers, low in his saddle, kept pace with Pony. He was, Amanda realized, trying to slide himself between Amanda and the enemy, pushing Pony toward Smitty and the front of the line. She heard a shot and a single shout of pain; one of the brothers had been hit. They were nearly to the rocks when more shots rang out. An intense pain burned across her side. Her hand automatically went to cover it and came away bloody.

CHAPTER 4

O*h, dear Lord*, Amanda thought. *I've been shot.* Raising her eyes from her wound, she saw Ayers looking at her over her shoulder. She wondered if she'd spoken the words out loud. The edges of her vision were rimmed with a feathery black that was creeping inward.

"Hang on," Ayers called, "Just hang on a little longer." She stiffened her resolve, not wanting him to think her weak. Why that mattered at this moment was beyond her, but it helped her to focus. Amanda stared at the spot between her horse's ears, the top of the head that bobbed with each stride.

Behind the rocks, Smitty pulled each horse and mule into a huddle. Mr. Ayers jumped off his horse as Smitty grabbed Pony's bridle. Ayers slipped an arm around Amanda's waist, gripping the uninjured side, and the other slipped under her thighs as he pulled her out of the saddle. Amanda hissed from the pain of movement and gripped his hand. He placed her on the ground, tucked between two rocks. He glanced at her side. "You'll be alright. Wait here."

Was she all right? She was unsure and scared and could only latch onto Ayers' words. She leaned against the granite, glad for the solid backing. She held her hand tight against her side and felt the warm wet blood seep between her fingers.

The rest of the train was in the circle now. Dick helped Richard off his horse. Scamp was trying to secure all the animals, even as they danced around in their fears. Mr. Ayers turned to Pastor Frank, whose hand shook around his gun.

"Put your gun away and help Miss Hildreth and Richard," Ayers bit out. Pastor Frank looked in turn at the blood on Amanda's side and on Richard's leg and turned pale and unsteady. "Oh, for Pete's sake."

Ayers turned back to Amanda. "Hold your kerchief on it to stop the flow. Hold it tight." She knew this. She, who had so often helped women injured by the mill machinery. She knew this.

Collect yourself, Amanda said to herself. She pulled her kerchief out of her pocket and pressed it to her side. It hurt. It burned. She took deep breaths. Despite the heat of the sun reflecting off the boulders—she could hardly believe it was still morning—she shivered.

Amanda looked around to distract herself. Dick was just finishing tying a kerchief on his injured brother's calf. He propped Richard against a rock. Guns in hand, both were now back at work. Dick crouched down and skittered over behind another rock. They chose their spots then began laying out caps and powder. Pastor Frank dropped behind an outcropping and looked to Ayers and Smitty for orders.

Smitty looked at the man, crouched so far back he wouldn't be much help in a gunfight. He said, "Why don't you say a prayer for us, Pastor?"

Pastor Frank looked shocked, but quickly gave a nod. He lowered his head for a moment, his hands held together in prayer. Then he looked up.

"Fight the good fight. God's wrath will avenge. And," he added, "The Lord trains your hands for battle. Amen."

This was not the prayer Amanda expected, and from the look of surprise on Smitty's face, it wasn't what he expected either.

Ayers squinted at the pastor, then turned to Smitty, who was climbing up on a rock. "Five minutes," said Ayers. Amanda watched him climb up the rock face, partially obscured—at least she hoped so—by the rustling leaves of several aspen trees. He had his old rifle hung off his shoulder by a strap. The fringe under his sleeves danced.

Smitty had propped his rifle on the rock. When Ayers approached an open spot, he shouted, "Now," and they all opened fire at the bad guys. Ayers was past the spot and now hidden from sight. Return shots had them ducking.

This went on for what seemed like forever. Several shots from one side when a target was spotted, and then a repeat from the other. And then, silence. Smitty relaxed a little, telling the others to keep eyes out. He stooped low and walked to Amanda.

"May I?" She nodded and removed her hand from her side. He gently peeled back the kerchief and looked at her wound. She did, too. Between the torn edges of her bodice fabric was a red line of oozing flesh along her ribcage. It was, essentially, a bad burn. Smitty's face lost some tension and boy did that make Amanda feel better.

"Just a crease, Miss Amanda. Once this is over, we'll get you cleaned up. You'll be better in no time." Amanda looked down at the raw flesh, still seeping blood. She tried to imagine what she'd say to someone if it weren't her own wound, but she couldn't think of anything encouraging. She knew her thoughts reflected on her face, because he added, "One step at a time, Miss Amanda."

Smitty next turned to check on the injury to Richard's leg. "Shot clean through," he said. Richard nodded but didn't look down. He was reloading his gun with powder and shot, and was angry. Pastor Frank looked a little miffed that the pack master hadn't checked on him. Dick was hunkered on a ledge, partway up the rock face, but obscured by a tree. He was still looking for signs of their attackers but took a moment to give Smitty a thumbs-up.

Finally, Smitty turned to Scamp and together they started checking the animals. First, they checked Richard's horse. Amanda saw Smitty fingering a hole in the pack and lifting it to check the horse underneath. The horse was untouched. Scamp opened the pack and pulled out a tin can of beans, shot through one side and leaking sauce. He gave it to Smitty who turned and tossed it to Richard.

"Bet you'll like beans a bit more after this." Richard gave a quick smile. He placed the can on the ground and turned back to his lookout.

Smitty and Scamp moved from horse to mule to horse, finding no other injuries. Smitty checked his watch and went back to his rocky perch. He checked it again and then, with a notice to the others, they each set off one shot high above the heads of the enemy. That caused return shots, and in the pause when those men would have been reloading, a shot came from just north of them. Amanda guessed that was Calvin, catching the other side unprepared. Swiftly another shot came, and then another.

She couldn't imagine how he was reloading so quickly. They heard shouts, another shot, and then—nothing.

After the initial shock, after the shooting had ended, Amanda began to calm down. Her hands stopped shaking and her wound had stopped bleeding, mostly. Using her kerchief and water from a canteen handed to her by Smitty—she really couldn't think of him as Mr. Smith anymore—she sponged off her side. She lifted the side of her blouse and tied a clean cloth against the raw flesh. It wasn't deep, she could see. She'd seen worse from accidents at the mill in Lowell.

Smitty and Dick were checking their animals over, and laughing now and again. Richard finally sat down to tend to his own wound. Pastor Frank leaned against a rock, wringing his hands. Several times he stood to peer in the direction of the men who'd attacked them. Scamp had that over-excited look of a youth who didn't fully understand how bad the danger had been. They all kept their weapons ready at their sides, she noticed.

Amanda stood and went to Pony. Smitty had already checked the horse over, but she needed something to do. She ran her hands over his shoulders and chest, tweaked his ears and rubbed his nose. She patted his hindquarters and leaned over as she ran her hands down his legs. She saw a few new scratches from the run through the sagebrush, but nothing serious. When she straightened back up, she felt a sharp burn in her side that caused her to cover her wound with her hands.

She was immediately distracted by the presence of Calvin beside her. He looked disheveled and tired but was apparently uninjured. Cal offered her a small smile. "You are one strong woman, up and checking your horse already. Are you sure you're from the city?"

Amanda smiled back, this time the heat in her cheeks not unwelcome. "We breed 'em tough in my family."

Cal laughed, then turned earnest. "Would you like me to look at your wound? I'm good with healing. I've had my fair share."

"Oh no," Amanda said. "I'm fine."

"I have two sisters, you know. I won't give you any trouble."

"Oh, thank you," Amanda said, realizing he thought she was being modest, which she was, but only some. "It's not as bad as it seemed at first. I helped a lot with injuries at the mill where I used to work… I can care for it myself."

Then neither said anything and, somehow, they were just

gazing into each other's eyes, brought back to reality only when Pony began shifting about trying to reach a tuft of grass.

"May I ask you something?" asked Amanda. Cal nodded.

"How did you fire that old rifle so quickly? We could hear it."

Cal pulled his rifle off the rock he'd leaned it up against. He held it out with one hand, pointing to the hardware with his other.

"I altered it. See this copper tube I added. It's for a percussion cap. And this here hammer I modified?"

"That's a lot faster than a powder charge, then?"

"Heaps faster." He slung his rifle over his shoulder. Then, Cal gave a tip of his imaginary hat, a smooth move that Amanda would expect to see on a man with a fancy beaver felt top hat and a vest and coat. Not a mountain man. He turned away and walked to Smitty who was crouched next to Richard, examining his leg. Amanda took a deep breath and tried to find something else to stare at. But she couldn't stop herself from listening to Cal, no—Mr. Ayers and Smitty—Mr. Smith. From the looks of it, all the men were trying to listen in, too.

"Thank you, Cal," said Smitty. "How'd it go?"

"Three men, one badly injured. The other two ran for it."

"What about the injured man?"

"One of his own took care of him."

Amanda couldn't help but look over at the men then. A look of disgust crossed over Smitty's face, matching the tone of Cal's voice.

Oh, my, thought Amanda.

"What did he look like?" asked Pastor Frank.

"Does it matter?" asked Cal.

The pastor gave a slight shake of his head.

"Did you recognize them?" asked Smitty.

"No. Whites, though. Not Indians," said Cal.

Smitty paused to consider that. "Did they get your packhorse?"

"No," said Cal, "no interest, it seemed. They wanted something on this train."

They looked at each other, at the trees, at the horses, at their belt buckles, but not at Amanda.

CHAPTER 5

Calvin was more attuned to Miss Amanda than he should have been on such short acquaintance. So, despite her apparent interest in the line of packhorses stretching their necks here and there to reach something to eat, he could tell by her stillness how she strained to hear what he had to say to Smitty. He drew the pack master across the clearing and made a show of holding his gun out, flat on his hand, as though to show it off.

"You know something," he said to Smitty quietly.

"Not exactly," said Smitty, taking the gun into his own hands and checking the barrel. "I had a feeling we were being watched, but I wasn't sure… coulda been Crow or Sioux, not happy we're in their territory." He gave a little shrug.

Cal gave a snort that wasn't quite laughter. *Not happy*—what an understatement. Even with all the land granted to the whites, they still wanted more. Even if, in this case, it was just to pass through. But as they did so, Smitty's stock foraged for grass and the men hunted for themselves, and every bit they took was less for the tribes.

Smitty ignored Cal's outburst. "But they were good enough

at laying low." He handed the gun back and continued. "This is far off the beaten path for a regular robbery. More opportunities coming from the south." He looked at Cal and then over at Amanda.

She had given up trying to overhear them and was fending off the attentions of Pastor Frank.

"I did wonder about Miss Amanda," said Cal. "What do you know about her? Is she with that pastor?" He had noted the proprietary behavior of the man earlier, and his hovering concern for Amanda now, though she hadn't responded in kind. Not either time.

Cal realized his first question was for Smitty, for their investigation of the attack, but the second was for himself. What could he say? A beautiful young woman was bound to attract attention anywhere, but out here... well.

Smitty spared a glance at the young woman and then turned to a mule. He bent at the waist, running his hand down the mule's front leg until he reached the hoof. He leaned into the animal until it raised its bent leg. Cal leaned in to hear him.

"She's traveling alone. Don't know how she made it so far without trouble."

"How far?"

"Some city in Massachusetts."

Cal gave a low whistle. He was impressed.

"I found Miss Amanda at Fort Laramie. She had a place on a wagon train heading for Utah on the Oregon Trail. Once there, she was going to head north to Montana Territory. She was hired back East by a fellow to care for his wife who was in the family way. Damn fool should have left her back East." Smitty glared at the hoof.

"That woman had two babies, too early. They got sick in Nebraska Territory and they stayed at the fort when the rest of the wagon train moved on. Well, the gal and babies died. Miss

Amanda didn't want to continue on with the fellow alone. So I let her come along."

Cal knew Smitty to be a genuinely kind man, but not one to necessarily seek out strangers to help. The older man had pulled out a knife and was trimming the cracked hoof. Smitty did not look up, but Cal could see by the slightest upturn of the corner of his mouth that Smitty enjoyed making Cal draw the details out of him. Neither man was keen on gossip, but then, neither was it common to find a beautiful, unattached young woman out in the wilds.

Cal gave up. He couldn't hide his interest, and Smitty had recognized it almost before he did. "Alright, old timer, how'd she end up with you?"

Smitty let the hoof go and stood up. His lip curled. "Pastor Frank brought her over. He heard she was looking for work to get her to Virginia City, to her brother, and that a couple of fellows were planning to help her 'work' her way across the mountains. I didn't get the impression they were going to give her much choice."

Cal felt an anger rise up inside him.

"Up near Fort Benton, I might have passed her on to that preacher's family running the Sun River Indian Farm. But round Fort Kearney, I couldn't think of anyplace she'd be safe long enough to get word to her stepbrother."

Smitty put the hoof down, and with one hand on his back, straightened up with a groan. "That has got to be one of my least favorite jobs."

Cal reached over and took the hoof paring knife from Smitty. He walked around the mule's head to the other side of it. He ran his hand down the other foreleg and pinched the ankle until the animal shifted its weight, and bent its knee to raise the foot for him. As he ran the paring knife around, trimming and leveling the hoof, he found a wave of disgust had come to accompany the anger. This was the problem with the westward rush. So many men, all outside the bounds of civilization, letting their basest instincts take over. He knew a woman like this would be in high demand, even from the decent ones.

He let the mule's hoof down and handed the knife back to Smitty. The wind was picking up and he looked up to see clouds pushing up from the valley south of them.

"And the preacher?"

Smitty gave a low chuckle. "She doesn't seem too interested in him."

Cal liked hearing that, but he still didn't like what had just happened. "Well, someone sure seems interested in her."

Smitty was watching him intently. "I have no reason to think Miss Amanda was the object of those desperados. But either way, I don't think she'd fair well if we ended up on the losing side of a shootout." He paused a moment and then poked Cal in the middle of the chest. "You're going to take her."

"Pardon? Take her where?"

"These fellows might come back. They know we'll continue on the Bozeman Trail to get over the pass. But you know how to get to town without being seen. Meet us in Bozeman in a few days. I'll take Miss Amanda on to Virginia City from there."

Cal inhaled sharply. He did *not* like this idea. It could ruin everything.

"I need to get to Gallatin City quickly. I can't take an injured gal through the wilderness." *Even if she's pretty*, ran through his mind.

"She'll be safer with you, Cal. Her injury's not so bad. You can move faster than I can with this string of mules. Plus, how will either of us feel if she stays with me and something terrible happens?"

CHAPTER 6

"Y"ou need to go with Calvin, Miss Amanda," said Mr. Smith—he was not Smitty any longer.

"Go with Cal—Mr. Ayers? No." Amanda folded her arms across her chest but didn't elaborate. One thing she'd learned from being on her own was that giving an explanation was the same as giving the other person an opportunity to change her mind.

"Why yes, Miss Amanda." He turned his crinkled eyes into hers. "You see, this is my pack train and I decide who rides with me." Scamp stood nearby, goggle-eyed.

"No!" She forgot her own rule. "You promised me to Virginia City if I worked my way. You can't just leave me!"

"I'm not leaving you. I'm sending you on a safer route." When Amanda tried to interrupt, Smitty held up his hand and his voice turned sterner. "I allowed you to ride along at a greatly reduced fee because I was concerned for your safety if you stayed in Fort Laramie, or continued on with that emigrant wagon train, or tried to make it to Montana Territory on your own. A pretty young girl with no money. What if it were my daughter out there?"

Amanda wanted to argue but she knew this was true. She had very little money and it was only because she'd been hired to help Geraldine that she'd been able to travel west without family or friends. But when Geraldine and the babies caught the cholera, there was nothing she could do. She couldn't—or rather wouldn't—travel farther with Geraldine's widower.

But how could he think sending her off with some wild Mountain Man was *safer*? They couldn't think these bandits were coming back for her? "But—"

"But nothing," said Smitty. "I was concerned for your safety and I still am. You'll be safer out in the trees with Cal than trotting down the open trail with me."

Amanda didn't know how to respond. The open trail wasn't a heck of a lot better than a deer path. Now, Smitty wanted her to go off on an *actual* deer path. And Calvin Ayers was more of a stranger than Smitty or any of the men in the pack train. She'd known them for a few weeks, at least. Smitty clearly trusted Ayers and Scamp idolized him, but she sure didn't want to travel into the unknown mountains with some unknown man, with bandits on their trail.

Amanda felt anger and frustration boiling up inside of her. A man had forced her to leave the mill and head west. Another man had forced her to leave the wagon train for this pack mule train. And now these men were forcing her off the trail and out into the wilderness with a… a… mountain man! When could a woman take charge of her own destiny?

Amanda looked at the striking landscape, listened to the rustling aspen leaves and felt the wind against her skin. It didn't really matter, she thought resignedly, she had nowhere to go but forward. She turned to Smitty again, but before she could speak, Calvin's voice cut in.

"I didn't know the men, but they seemed determined. They might return with reinforcements. Now is our chance to spirit you away where they can't find you."

So much for suspicions, she thought. There were men out there, bad men, willing to shoot and kill to get at her. This had never been a problem in Lowell. Her thoughts must have shown her fear because he continued. "I'm not keeping you, Miss Amanda. I'll get you to your brother safely, just by a different route."

His tone and words were sympathetic, but she still didn't know this man. Yes, he had a handsome quality under his mountain man trappings and was kind to her when she was injured, but that wasn't a reason to trust her life in his hands. He was big and strong...and she was alone.

"Mr. Smith..." she was appealing to a man she barely knew. "Why..."

"Miss Amanda." Mr. Smith took a deep breath but there was no uncertainty in his voice. "It'll be safer for all if you go with Mr. Ayers."

"Surely I'll be safer with four men?" At a look from Scamp, she revised, "Five men?"

Smitty looked at young Scamp, the injured Richard, and the less than useful Pastor Frank. "Not this time."

And that ended the discussion. How could she insist on choosing her way when she wasn't even a paying customer? She had no one to back her up. Richard and Dick weren't paying much attention to her predicament. Scamp seemed envious of her chance to ride off with Mr. Ayers. Only Pastor Frank seemed to dislike the idea of Amanda riding off into the wilderness with a mountain man.

"I fear Miss Amanda is going from the frying pan to the fire." He looked dolefully at Mr. Ayers. Amanda wasn't sure if he was concerned about her physical or moral virtue. Suddenly, his eyes lit up and he gave a satisfied smile. "I'll go with you, Miss Amanda."

Amanda felt a leap of gratitude inside of her, which was quickly squashed by Cal's quick response.

"Absolutely not."

His voice was so determined that she knew he was not going to relent. Pastor Frank looked angry, but he didn't argue.

Amanda felt more scared now than in the gunfight. Then, she'd been a bystander, hunkered down while others fought. Now, she was in the thick of it. How she wished she could escape this madness. She'd like to be delivered to her step-brother's doorstep with a snap of her fingers. Or back to the familiarity, and relative safety, of Lowell. Or even to her father's farm. But there was no policeman walking his beat to whom she could call out, no friendly neighbors to appeal to.

Amanda took a deep breath.

"Let's go then," she said and turned toward Pony. She didn't want to look at this group of men, to let them see how close to tears she was.

"No, Miss," said Mr. Ayers. "We'll leave Pony with the pack train. If they're following and see the tracks veer off, they'll know where you turned off and where to start to follow. This way, it'll be a little longer before they realize you're gone."

He walked over to the horse and unhitched the ropes holding her two small satchels to the saddle. He nodded to Smitty and Scamp, "See you in Bozeman."

"Follow me," he said to Amanda. He led her to his horse. It was a large brown mare with black socks, mane and tail. "My pack horse is at full weight, and I don't have an extra saddle, anyway. You'll have to ride Miss Molly with me."

She looked up at the saddle and the rolled blanket tied to the back of it with three leather straps. What could she say, in the woods at the foothills of a huge mountain range with a stranger who claimed he would protect her? She nodded. She had so many words and emotions boiling and roiling inside of her, but feared if she opened her mouth, they'd burst out in an incoherent mess that wouldn't help her anyway.

Amanda swiveled her head to Smitty, who gave her an

encouraging nod. She looked to Frank, who gave her a discouraging shake of the head, and to Scamp, who smiled like this was all perfectly regular.

Calvin finished tying on her satchels. He mounted the horse and then held his hand down to Amanda. "I'll pull you up behind me." She put her foot on his stirruped foot and gave him her hand. He pulled her straight up and then twisted to drop her behind his back. She grabbed onto his waist. It felt so strange, so intimate. She gripped with one hand while she adjusted her skirts with the other. It might feel intimate, she thought, but it wasn't. She yanked the material down to cover her right calf.

And with that, she narrated to herself. *And so, Amanda Hildreth left the pack train to ride off into a new part of the wilderness on a horse named Miss Molly, with a scruffy mountain man named Calvin Ayers.*

CHAPTER 7

Calvin and Amanda rode along a path barely
qualifying for the name. Through the trees and brush,
Calvin navigated his horse so subtly that Amanda
couldn't tell he was actually doing anything. Maybe his horse
knew the route all by itself? The packhorse, tied by a long rope
to the lead horse, walked along behind, its only goal seeming to
be to nibble at any edibles it spotted en route.

The afternoon wore on, the sun hot overhead. When they
rode in the shade, Amanda was comfortably warm. When they
rode in the sun, she was terribly hot. The difference between
the shade and the sun, well, it was quite a bit more of a difference than at home.

The heat and the swaying of the horse, combined with the
passing of the thrill of their battle, left Amanda exhausted. She
kept drifting off, to awaken when the horse stumbled or in
some way jarred her. She was barely aware of a rustling to the
side of the trail when a blue grouse shot up into the air.
Calvin's horse gave a small sideways hop away from it in a
nervous response. Amanda, unprepared, tipped backward and
rolled right off the back of the horse.

She landed on her own rump, legs splayed out in front of her. The impact had jarred the wind right out of her.

The horses stopped immediately; Calvin was down off his horse in a bound and right there at her side. "Are you hurt?"

She wasn't, and she knew that he knew she wasn't—and it was only his hint of a smile that told her he wanted to laugh. She felt aggravated that he was laughing at her again but appreciated how he was only snickering on the inside.

"No, I don't think so," she said primly, as though she'd just turned her ankle on a walk in the park. And then the horse behind her blew a wet breath along her cheek. She gave a wry smile. "Only my pride," she said. She thought of how Cal had spied her in the woods outside of Smitty's camp. For a moment, she wondered how many more embarrassing situations she'd have with Cal as witness.

Calvin returned her smile and said, "Your side? Does it hurt?"

"It burns a little, but it's tolerable," she said. Amanda couldn't help but appreciate his concern. And how the skin around his eyes crinkled when he smiled. She tried not to blush.

He stood and held out his hand to help her up. This time, he held out his locked hands so she could step on them to mount the horse. He grabbed her skirts and helped yank them down to make her modest again, then mounted with a high swing of his leg so he didn't kick her. "Put both of your hands around my waist." She did so, and with his left hand across his front, he gripped her right forearm. With his right hand, he directed the horse through the reins and clenched his legs to start moving. This time, secure, Amanda stayed on the horse with greater ease.

They walked through the woods quietly, the horses one behind the other. At one opening in the trees, Cal pointed down the valley to a heard of small pronghorn antelope grazing among the sagebrush and long grass.

"Are women in such short supply then?" Amanda asked.

"What?"

"That we're kidnapped upon sight? That men lay in wait of emigrant trains looking for women?" She highly doubted this was the case, but what the case was, she just didn't know.

"No, not usually."

That triggered an alarm in Amanda. Her arm must have tensed because she felt Cal pat her wrist.

"I shouldn't joke at a time like this, sorry."

"No, you shouldn't," she said. Amanda wished she could pull back from him, but didn't want to roll off the horse again. She waited, and realized he wasn't going to her answer her real question. "Please tell me what's going on."

"I'm not certain." Cal paused. "Are you an heiress in disguise?"

"Oh, hardly that!"

"Other than your brother, what connections do you have out here?"

"Only Samuel, my stepbrother. He owns a mercantile store in Virginia City. I'm going to work for him."

"Samuel, huh?" Cal paused again, considering. "I know Virginia City fairly well. I can't say I am acquainted with a Samuel with that kind of store."

"I've heard there are ten thousand people there. Surely you don't claim to know them all?"

Amanda believed Calvin was trying to help her, but even so, her hackles were up. He was asking questions as though this mess was her fault entirely.

"The city's grown by leaps and bounds, you're right. And there's lots of men coming and going. I could very well have overlooked it." Cal didn't seem as if he believed this, but what could Amanda say? If men didn't go kidnapping women at random, and if Samuel was indeed her only local connection, then it stood to reason she and Samuel did indeed play a role in this mystery.

Amanda was bewildered. Her brother was a successful storekeeper in Virginia City. She was an ex-millworker of unexceptional background emigrating to a new life in Montana Territory. Surely there was an explanation to that shoot-out that did not connect to them?

She thought of the last time she'd seen Samuel. She had been back to the farm for a Sunday dinner with her family; Samuel had shown up there unexpectedly. Watching through the window, Amanda had seen him arrive on a rented hack from town. He'd ridden with slumped shoulders and an equally slumped face. At the hitching ring on the side of the barn, he stopped the horse. After a moment, he wiped his face with his hands, squared his shoulders, and dismounted. By the time he entered the house, he was strutting like a rooster, proudly announcing his plan to head west to start a new life. He hoped to start his own store out where business was booming.

"I'm done working for someone else," he'd said to her father and stepmother. Then he'd turned to Amanda. "And you should be too, Amanda. Don't waste your life in the mill. Head out West—where there's opportunity for anyone."

Everyone had laughed at the idea of a young, unmarried woman heading West to make her fortunes on her own. Everyone, that is, but her.

CAL FELT… AWKWARD. THAT WAS THE ONLY WAY HE COULD

think to phrase it. Or maybe, *uncomfortable*. That worked, too. Here he was, leading a pretty, young woman alone into the mountains. At the moment, her breasts were pressed up against his back, and so was the side of her face. He was gripping her forearm carefully; he could tell from her slackened grip and slow, steady breathing that she was asleep again. The excitement of the shootout—and of getting shot—had quite worn her out.

Riding along the narrow deer trail with Amanda at his back was strangely nice. She sat behind the lip of the saddle, so her legs didn't run along his, but her feet would gently kick into his calves and ankles sometimes. Her arms around his waist were warm and firm.

He didn't know her. He didn't know if she was telling the truth about herself and her stepbrother. But he was inclined to believe her. Smitty had traveled with her for a few weeks and had vouchsafed her, too. She was forthright and pretty, and she'd handled this whole situation calmly. And, quite simply, he just wanted to believe in her.

Cal admitted to himself that he'd felt more... feelings... than he would have expected to feel, seeing the blood from her side seeping through her fingers, and the pale, scared face that had looked from the wound and then up to his own face. *This is why women shouldn't travel alone*, he'd thought. Once a man starts protecting something, or someone, he's going to feel responsible.

He'd wanted to comfort her, protect her, hold her.

And that's where the trouble had started.

He didn't know what was going on, so he had to be on the lookout for anyone, anywhere. All he knew was that someone was after her, and for some reason. It was likely related to her stepbrother, which did not bode well for her future plans working alongside this Samuel.

And so, he thought he should probably keep this whole trip

quiet; if some more men found out, her life might even be in jeopardy. Or at least her virtue. And if he and Smitty were wrong about the situation, and other people found out she'd traveled not just with a pack train of men alone, but then also with Cal—alone again, and in the middle of nowhere—her moral standing would be in question. Now, people were a whole lot more easygoing about those things out West, but it was still best not to poke the bear.

There were plenty of men who'd be interested in pretty Miss Amanda anyway, even the marrying kind of men, but Cal knew she'd be better off establishing herself on her own best terms. With or without her brother.

He had a pretty good reputation himself but knew he might lose it because of Miss Amanda. This misadventure was already perilously close to colliding with his own plans; he'd better start asking her more questions. Perhaps he could figure this out before they got to town and then he could hand her back to Smitty in good conscience.

Just then, his horse's ears twitched forward and the mare raised her head. He pinned Amanda's left arm more tightly under his own and pulled back on the reins with his left hand. At the same time, he grabbed his gun with his right hand.

Cal pulled up short when he saw a bear ahead, next to the trail, foraging. It was big and brown, dappled in the shadows of the spruce trees. The bear paused and lifted its huge head in their direction. It didn't seem to be raising its hackles at the sight of them, but neither did it move on.

Amanda slept on. Here he was, trying to figure out how to help her, and she was just dozing away, no care about the dangers of the wilderness and no care either about what could happen to her when she got to town. Cal felt himself getting angry.

He'd provide Amanda with a reminder of the dangers of

traveling the wilderness. Maybe she could begin to realize she wasn't just inconveniencing the men around her. He tugged on Amanda's arm and whispered her name. He hoped she didn't scream or the bear might charge them.

CHAPTER 8

Amanda awoke with a start, jerking backward. Cal was glad he'd pinned her arm under his own. Before she could speak, he gave jerk of his head and whispered, "Look over there."

She peeked over his shoulder and said, "Oh!" Her eyes were round. Cal waited to hear the fear in her voice. "A brown bear. He's so big," she whispered. He heard the awe in her voice, instead.

"See that big hump on his shoulders? That's a grizzly." That ought to help her realize the gravity of the situation.

"What's he eating?" she asked almost under her breath.

Eating? So, she wasn't scared at all.

"What's he eating?" she whispered again.

"Huckleberries," he said. Well, so much for scaring her. They stayed still and watched the bear nosing around the low bushes.

"I've heard of them. How do they taste?"

How do they taste? Clearly, the woman had no sense of the risks of being in the woods with wild animals. He was annoyed by this, but… he could hear and sense her appreciation for all the nature surrounding them. He felt it, too, shared in it. It made a change to share his love of this wilderness with a pretty woman. With this pretty woman.

"Delicious. A lot like blueberries."

She was so close to him now, leaning in to see the bear more closely… so close, he could feel her nod against his shoulder and pick up the warmth of her face on his own skin. Cal knew they should move on, but he was taken by Amanda's awe. His horses were not so taken, and Miss Molly shifted under them. Amanda gripped his sides with both arms, and whispered, "How do we know it won't attack?"

He chuckled quietly, glad she had an ounce of sense. "The bear's more interested in eating, but we won't push our luck." He knew there was another trail just over the ridge. He holstered his gun and turned his horse into the woods.

"You're certain he won't follow us?" Amanda whispered.

Cal grit his teeth. She didn't know beans about these woods and bears. He'd been living in the area for a decade, but still, she doubted him.

"Yes. That bear was content with its berries. Just remember, back away from a bear quietly." He reached out an arm to push a branch out of their way.

"Is that what I should do for all wild animals?"

Cal felt a wave of relief that Amanda was concerned about her own safety. And, perhaps, a little pride that she trusted him to advise her. "No. Yell real loud and wave your arms if you see a mountain lion."

"That will scare it away?"

"Well, probably not. If you see the mountain lion, it's probably too late anyway."

"Are you teasing me?"

"No, ma'am."

"Oh." Amanda tightened her arms around his ribs. "How about a… a moose?"

"Miss Amanda, if you have a moose with his dander up, you had better get out of the way!"

֍

A FEW HOURS LATER, CAL STOPPED THEIR TWO-HORSE PACK train at a slight clearing in the trees. It was not open enough to be a meadow, but flat and not overly covered with brush and bushes.

"Already?" asked Amanda. "It's still plenty light out."

Cal twisted in the saddle to look her in the face.

"I know you want to get to your brother, but this spot's clear... some grass for the animals, and there's a creek just past those trees over there. It's probably half seven and my animals need rest."

Cal dismounted and offered his hand to Amanda. She gave a tentative smile as she took his hand and slid off the horse. She liked how Cal would answer all her questions even though he seemed annoyed some of the time. She was learning so much about how to live out there—like a mountain woman. She felt the corners of her mouth turn up at her silliness. To distract herself, she offered to gather firewood.

"No need for a fire." Cal gave a sigh and began to unpack his horses. "We don't want to draw attention. And we certainly don't need the heat or light."

Amanda didn't want to think about the attention they didn't want to attract. She began to untie the small bags off the horse. "I'm still not used to how late the light lasts out here. Even after the late sunsets."

Cal took the satchel from her and carried it over to set under a tall lodgepole pine. "Only in summer."

After unpacking, feeding and watering the horses, they sat on a fallen log to eat their own meal. With no fire to cook over, they ate hardtack and leftover cornbread Cal had tucked away.

"I wish we had some of those huckleberries," said Amanda.

Cal nodded. "They'd be a good addition to dinner."

They ate off their tin plates quietly for a few minutes. Then Cal spoke.

"So, what happened? Your brother didn't send you enough money to get to Virginia City?" He didn't sound too impressed by that thought.

Amanda didn't want him to think badly of her stepbrother. "Oh, no! That's not it at all. He's been sending money to my father and stepmother for a while now, to pay back a loan from my father. But I…" She paused a moment, realizing how foolish she was going to sound. "I didn't tell him I was coming."

Cal raised his eyebrows at her.

"I should say, I sent him a letter, but then I left only a few days later. Of course, there was no time for him to respond. Nor, I admit, did I mind avoiding a possible *no*."

Samuel could be carefree and flippant. Amanda knew he might tell her that despite telling her to head West, he hadn't really meant it. Well, he'd had his opportunity to start over when he needed to, and she wanted hers. She thought of how she'd written to the mill owner, telling him about the unsafe practices at the mill that led to women getting injured, sometimes terribly. The only response she'd received was an angry grip on the shoulders from the foreman, a grip that left bruises. She'd known then that her time at the mill was coming to a rapid close.

She paused for a bite of cornbread and realized Cal was looking at her like she had two heads. She decided to change the subject. "I didn't understand how different things were out here. Smaller and bigger."

Cal watched her intently. He seemed genuinely interested in her assessment. "Smaller and bigger, Miss Amanda?"

"Well, the towns are so much smaller. Lowell, where I've been living these past few years, has more than 35,000 people it."

Cal gasped. "Virginia City is the biggest city I've ever been in and it has ten thousand people or so. It is crazy and wild, and I can't imagine something more than three times bigger." He shook his head at the wonder of it.

Amanda leaned forward, smiling. "I know what you mean. I've been to Boston, twice, and they say it has more than *150,000* people!" She nodded in agreement when Cal gave a low whistle.

"But out here, if I even see a town, it's so tiny. Scores of people, maybe hundreds, but not tens of thousands. Yet, the land is so much bigger. The mountains are bigger. The rivers are bigger. The flatlands—the prairies—are bigger. Even the spaces between them all are bigger!" She reached over to take his plate, inadvertently brushing his fingers lightly with hers. With a slight blush, she stood.

"It's spectacular. Sublime," she said, looking around. "But not, I now realize, a place to come poorly prepared." She turned to take the plates to the creek to rinse. She might as well blush again. "That's why you're so fascinating. So self-sufficient and capable, alone in the mountains."

Amanda tucked her head down as she knelt on the rocks at the side of the creek. She rubbed the two plates with the river gravel and hoped Cal, leaning against a tree nearby, wasn't paying attention to her. She knew she was being a bit forward, but not until she said it aloud did she realize how much. She snuck a look and realized he was scanning the treeline. Instead of being relieved, she felt let down. Well, perhaps she wasn't so interesting to him if he hadn't even noticed what she'd said. That bothered her more than she would have expected. She was feeling a strange mix of embarrassment and disappointment.

She shook the crumbs off the napkin that had wrapped the cornbread and used it to dry the plates, subdued. She stood, and then headed back to their camp. Cal walked up beside her.

"I've another question for you if you don't mind."

She was so glad he didn't bring up her last statement that she rushed to say, "Not at all." What was it about this man that made her so inclined to spill her beans?

"How come you're so good with wounds? Not many women are so calm about getting shot and then dressing the wound after. Not Yankee city girls, especially."

"Do you know many Yankee city girls?" she laughed.

He smiled and his eyes crinkled in the corners. "Not so many."

Amanda handed the plates to Cal so that he could pack them. She chose a downed tree trunk to sit on, looking west through the trees at the setting sun.

"I grew up on a farm, with lots of animals and some brothers and sisters. That was the start of it. Just helping out and learning from my mother and father." Cal sat down on the ground opposite her, resting his arms on his raised knees. He alternated watching her with scanning the woods and animals. "Later, I went to work in a mill in Lowell. We were making fabric on big machine looms. It wasn't uncommon for a girl to get a cut, or a rope burn from the machines. So I became known for helping with small wounds."

She looked down at her clasped hands but soon saw only the mill. "And sometimes, there were big accidents or fires. I helped until a doctor could be fetched. Or a priest." She fell silent.

Amanda looked up to see Cal watching her with a crease between his eyes. He was concerned. "And these were all women working in this mill?"

Oh, dear, she thought. *He's one of those, then, concerned only about the jobs the men didn't get to have!*

"The men weren't there. They'd all gone off to the war," she said carefully.

"No, I get that. I just wondered about having all the women working in such an unsafe place. I guess I understand a little better why you weren't so scared to come out here. If you take the shooters and the bears out of it, it's much safer here." Cal grinned at her. There was even a hint of admiration in his expression.

Amanda was flabbergasted. He did get it! At least, a big part of it.

"Yes! At least here, the danger won't be for someone else's profit. Well, mostly…" She thought about the ambush earlier and what the men had wanted her for.

Cal nodded. "You're going to fit in fine if you choose to."

Amanda smiled. After the many 'are you crazy?' comments and all the looks she'd received since she'd announced and started this journey, it sure felt good to be getting some approval at last.

"Did you fight in the War?" she asked.

She felt bold putting the question out there and could scarcely believe she'd said it. The farther west she traveled, the more people didn't want to even talk about it.

"No, I didn't." Cal watched her and she suspected he was gauging how much to tell her. "I was deep in the backcountry for a number of months. I didn't even know there was a war until it was five months gone on."

He swept his arm out, encompassing the mountains around them. "I've been out here for ten years, Miss Amanda," he said. "Been here since it was Oregon Territory, then Washington Territory, then Idaho Territory. Now it's Montana Territory. They keep changing the lines and the names, but it's all the same to me; it's my home. And I don't feel any connection to Missouri, where I was born, or really anything back East."

He took a deep breath. "But in the end, what decided me

was that I had some brothers fighting for one side, and cousins for the other, and I couldn't bear the idea of shooting at any one of them, Miss."

Amanda wasn't sure how to respond, but Cal prevented the need. He rolled up off the ground in a smooth move. "That war, thankfully, is over."

Cal held out his hand to Amanda. It was warm and calloused. "Let's get ready for sleep. I'd like us to get up and moving early tomorrow." He pulled her gently to a standing position. After a moment, he released her hand and turned to pull bedrolls from a pack.

CAL WOKE AMANDA AT SUNRISE. THE SUN HAD NOT YET risen over the mountains, but the sky to the east was pink and the stars above were fading. The air was cool and crisp.

He gave Amanda a drink of water, offered her a moment of privacy, then hustled her onto the horse.

They'd pushed hard yesterday, but he could only do so much when his horse was hauling two. He didn't want to founder Miss Molly. Amanda had held up well the day before and hadn't complained, even when he could see she was flagging. Crossing the country was hard, most certainly, but a slow and steady pack train across the plains was not the same as a fast-paced ride through the mountains with a gunshot wound.

Cal still didn't understand why she was getting so much attention. He thought that unless she was completely fooling him, she truly didn't know what was going on. And that led Cal back to the stepbrother; what could Samuel be up to that made his sister of such interest? Amanda was interesting enough on her own, but that didn't usually lead to shoot-outs or attempted kidnappings.

Amanda's arms were loose around his sides and she

brushed against him with the rhythm of the horse. He kept his left arm tight over hers; he didn't want her to fall off again and smiled at the thought.

"How's your side?" He felt the momentary clutch of her hands. "Did I wake you? I'm sorry."

"No, I was in my own head, is all."

"What was happening in there?"

He heard her chuckle. "You might think not much," she said, "but my head won't turn off right now."

There was a pause. He waited, wondering if she'd like to tell him. He found that he wanted to know.

After a few minutes of the gentle bump-bump of the horse's steady gait, Amanda spoke. "I was wondering about you, right when you spoke to me."

"Wondering what?"

"I was wondering how you became a mountain man. Were you a mountain baby with a mountain mama? I mean, there haven't been too many white folks out here for too long. At least, that's what I heard."

Cal laughed out loud. He had a vision of a baby suckling on a big grizzly bear sow. The way this gal thought, it just caused him no end of good humor.

He felt her arms relax when he laughed and knew she'd been hesitant to ask such a personal question. It was funny how riding along, back to front, with no eye contact, emboldened them each to ask and answer questions they might have avoided in a more proper setting. Well, he didn't mind her interest.

"I was born back East, in Missouri. My pa had a big farm with acres planned for all his sons. But my mother's brother, he came out here in 1855 on a fur trade expedition. He was hoping to establish a trading post for his company. It didn't pan out."

"Why not?"

"The fur trade was already dwindling then. Anyway, when the expedition was over I didn't want to go back." Cal paused for a moment, thinking back to his early days of adventure. "My older brothers… they married in their early twenties, took over their acreage, and started their families. That was not the life I was looking for."

He would have continued, but his horse raised her head and her ears stood at attention. He heard the horse behind him rustle in his nervousness.

"Whaa—?"

"Shhh," he whispered. He pulled Miss Molly to a halt, scanning around for the source of the animals' concern.

"What—?"

"Shhh," he whispered again, but too loudly.

After a few moments, the horses relaxed, trying instead to reach grass to munch.

Cal turned in the saddle to look directly at Amanda. "When I say, *shhh*, you *shhh*."

"I'm sorry. I only wanted to know what was going on," she said defensively.

Cal felt that angry frustration building up again. "What's going on," he said, "is that I told you to *shhh* and you didn't. Don't you have an ounce of self-preservation? You don't know how to survive in the wilds."

Amanda drew back, at least as far as she could when they were sharing a horse, and glared at him. "I'm not planning to live in the wilds. I'm planning to live in Virginia City."

Cal glared back. "You don't have a plan, Miss! You came out here on a whim. What if your stepbrother won't take you in? What do you do then, big city lady?"

"Then I'll find a job elsewhere and go live at the Women's Boarding House." She gave him a smirk. "There's one in Virginia City."

Cal was so startled by Amanda's response that for a

moment he didn't know what to say. And then, he started laughing. Hard. Amanda drew her brows down.

"What's so funny? That's a perfectly reasonable plan."

"No. No, it's not," he gasped through his laughs. Finally, he calmed down enough to say, "You see, that's not an actual boarding house. It's a whorehouse."

Amanda's face flamed red.

Cal pressed his knees and calves to get Miss Molly moving again and called out a low whistle to his packhorse. He was glad to be facing forward away from Amanda. She couldn't see that the smile had dropped from his face. He had allowed them to make too much noise with their arguing; he had forgotten, even if just for a moment, that she might be a hunted woman.

CHAPTER 9

The sun was well past midday when Calvin halted the horses. He held Amanda's arm as she slid off the horse onto shaky legs. When he released her, she tilted sideways and stumbled. How embarrassing!

After Cal dismounted he tied up the horses. He led Amanda off the trail a short way. She watched him as he observed everything around them. She was just wondering if there was a danger nearby when he turned back to the trail saying, "I'll leave you to your business."

How embarrassing, again! But, she realized, better than being overseen, like the last time and she appreciated a little space after their argument earlier. She completed her *business*, as Calvin had called it, and headed back to the main trail. Between the bear sighting and the fear of men chasing them down, she realized even this short separation from Cal bothered her. She hurried through the trees back to where she'd find him.

When she returned, the horses were still tied where they'd been left, but Cal was not there. She felt her pulse quicken and tried not to panic. Then, she heard his voice calling from the trees on the other side of the trail.

"Amanda! Over here."

She worked her way through some branches and brush, pulling at her skirt to find Cal standing in a patch of sun amidst low bushes that topped off just over his ankles. He reached over and took her hand. His own hand was warm. He turned hers and placed a dark blue berry in it; it looked like a large blueberry.

"Huckleberry. Try it."

It was a lot like a blueberry, just as he'd said earlier. It tasted sweet and with a hint of tartness. On the trail there had been fresh game and fish, dried fruits and canned goods, but very little when it came to fresh fruits or vegetables. She closed her eyes and savored it on her tongue. She opened her eyes to find Cal staring at her intently. She choked, swallowing the huckleberry by accident. He pounded her back as she coughed.

Amanda could feel the heat pouring off her face. "Um, delicious," she rasped out as she wiped the tears from her eyes. Cal was still watching her, but now with a combination of concern and amusement. His look before, well, she wasn't sure about that look, but it wasn't one she was used to. It made her feel nervous and excited, all at once.

"There's a spot near here where I usually lay a trap line in winter. I want to check out the animal activity while we're in the area. Perhaps you'd like to collect berries for tonight's supper while I do that?"

So, here she was, picking and eating firm, ripe huckleberries. She added some of them to a leather pouch Cal had given her. Standing in the dappled sun that reached down through the tall lodgepole pine trees, Amanda felt at peace for the first time since she'd realized her position at the mill would be lost if she didn't placate the foreman. She'd known she wouldn't do that, so she'd tried to find a job at a different mill… and soon learned she'd been blackballed at them all.

She'd been on the move a few months now, trying to get to Montana Territory. Since she hadn't the funds or the skills to travel alone, she'd found a position to work her way across the country. It hadn't been easy caring for the sickly and cranky Geraldine in a covered wagon while her unsettling husband hovered nearby.

Even after the death of Geraldine and her babies, Amanda had her plan to stick to, and her dream to lean on. With Smitty's help, she'd reach Virginia City and Samuel would welcome her with open arms. He'd give her a job and help her find a home. If not with him, then at a nice boarding house, or even find her a family with an extra room. Now, she was so close to all that but the recent events had made her question her expectations. At the very least, she doubted there even were many families with extra rooms. The nice women's boarding house might not exist either.

And, more importantly, if Samuel was in some kind of trouble, what could she do? She wasn't sure she could help herself. And even if he wasn't, she couldn't help but admit to herself that he might not welcome her warmly.

So, she wasn't in as much of a hurry to get there. She admitted to herself that it wouldn't change what was going to happen anyway. But this moment, given to her by Cal, was quiet and serene. She was going to savor it.

Amanda sighed and ate another berry. There was no point in gathering more; there was nowhere to store them all without too much mess, and no point in drawing the attention of the bears.

She whipped her head around. Something was coming up the path, something big pushing against the bushes and tree branches. She started to back out of the berry patch. How far away from the trail could she go—should she go—to avoid a wild animal and still find her way back to the trail later?

Her skirt caught. She ripped it free from a branch but stopped moving. Cal was due back anytime and she couldn't just leave him to run into a feeding bear.

Amanda looked around desperately. Noise! Smitty had said the bears would avoid her if she made noise. She found a stick as thick as her arm and started whacking the ground. Then she turned to a young evergreen and whacked at its trunk, over and over. With each thwack, she yelled louder and louder, "Go away, bear! Go away, bear!" It was part prayer.

Between the noises she was making and the blood rushing through her ears, Amanda didn't know if the bear was still coming or if she'd scared it off. She craned her neck around, trying to see if the bear was within sight. Keep noise-making?

Should she cut and run? Her heart pounded. She realized she hadn't dropped the leather pouch and instead, by gripping through it to the stick, had squashed all the berries. The red juice ran across her hands.

She shrieked when the bushes across the clearing rustled and spread open for a giant furry bear.

Only—it wasn't one.

A man halted, an amused smile barely visible through his bushy beard. He wore furs and skins, with a dirty canvas pack on his back. No wonder she'd thought he was a bear. This was a mountain man of the novels, but much bigger and way dirtier.

Amanda felt cross. It wasn't his fault she'd imagined a bear, but his sly smile told her he thought her panic was something to laugh at. She was scared and angry.

"You could have called out," she admonished the stranger.

He nodded, unabashed. "Didn't think you'd hear me for all the racket you was making."

That deflated Amanda a little. "Maybe so." She still didn't

like the amused way he was looking at her. She didn't like how he looked at her at all. Where was Cal? She tried to look unconcerned.

"Here for the berries?" she asked. "I've got enough for us," she tried to emphasize the *us*. "So you can take what you need."

She ignored his skeptical look as he eyed the sodden berry bag. She headed toward the trail. "Good day to you."

"No, ma'am. I'm not here for the berries. I'm looking for a woman and I think you might be her."

Amanda's blood froze in her veins and buzzed in her ears. There was no call for anyone to be looking for her out here. Did he mean *her* as in, Amanda, or as in any woman? It didn't look good for her in either case. She realized she'd stopped in place when the furry man had spoken. She was glad she still had her stick in hand, but what she really needed was Calvin. *Stall*, she told herself.

"How might that be?" She faced him squarely, hoping her face showed her confusion rather than her growing uneasiness.

"I'm looking for a pretty brown-haired gal. About your height and build, I was told. Samuel Emerson's sister. Aren't you his sister?"

"What?" She fumbled for a smooth response. "I'm afraid I don't know that gentleman. Has he sent you to find his sister?" If this man was there at her brother's bequest, she didn't want to lie to him, but her gut told her something was off. The man's response confirmed it.

"Ha! He isn't in a position to send anyone, anywhere."

Just then, more rustling in the wood, this time from the other direction. Amanda's heart took off racing again until she saw Cal striding toward her. He came right up and stood in front of her, his back to her and his front to the bear man. She reached forward to rest one hand upon the center of his back.

Just that touch and his presence made her feel safer.

"Can I help you?" Cal said to the man, in a tone that wouldn't have encouraged Amanda to say yes.

She peeked over Cal's shoulder. The bear man bristled, looking like he was trying to appear even bigger. "I recognize you, Ayers. I'm looking for Samuel Emerson's little sister. I'm looking on behalf of Ned Bart." This last was said with some implied menace, but it didn't mean anything to Amanda.

Cal visibly relaxed. He reached back as he spoke and took Amanda's hand. "Oh, then, you've got the wrong gal. This is my fiancée, fresh from Missouri."

Amanda tried not to look surprised. She held his hand and leaned up against his side as she imagined a frightened fiancée might do. As she wanted to do, as well.

Bear man stared at the two of them for a moment, then gave a nod. "I heard you left word at Gallatin Ferry that your gal might be arriving soon."

Amanda felt Cal stiffen slightly and suspected he was surprised this man knew this information. She was surprised, too, and surprised to find herself disappointed to learn of this *gal*, even at this tense moment.

Bear man turned his head a little, eyeing Amanda again. "You didn't come by way of the Missouri River, though." He let the sentence linger, implying something was wrong without accusing it. For all he looked like a big bear, this was no dummy.

But neither was Cal. He spoke bluntly. "This lady is mine. No business of yours how she arrived. You go find your lady someplace else." He pushed Amanda behind him again and spread his feet as if he was preparing for battle.

A little thrill ran through Amanda. It was ridiculously primitive, but Cal's words and tone made her feel protected and… special.

The possessive tone worked. Bear man laughed. "I'll keep

looking for my pretty. You can keep yours." He turned to head back the way he came.

"Hold on," said Cal. "You've got me curious." He placed his arm around Amanda and guided her to the narrow path from which he'd come. "The horses are along there, Sweetheart. I'll be along." He gave her a gentle shove and Amanda knew it was her chance to get away from the bear man.

She looked Cal in the eyes. What message was she trying to convey? *Be careful? Thank you? Don't shove me?* She truly didn't know.

CHAPTER 10

C al avoided filling Amanda in on what he'd learned
from the man dressed in bearskins, Ollie Linquist. Cal
had suspected who the man was by his reputation and
outfit, and it had been confirmed by his not-so-subtle threat
mentioning Ned Bart.

It was rumored that Bart had been part of the Innocents, a
group of road agents who'd stolen from and even murdered a
number of miners the year before. Bart had associated with
some of the men who'd been hung by the Vigilantes, but had
managed to avoid being named as part of the group. More
recent rumors had him starting up again in the Gallatin Valley,
just far enough from Virginia City to avoid notice.

Amanda's stepbrother was clearly in deep and, by association, so was Amanda. Cal hadn't been able to find out what
Emerson had done; he hadn't wanted to appear too interested.
But he'd learned that Ned Bart had this brother—and sister—
in his crosshairs. It was time he learned more about Amanda's
stepbrother. He didn't think she would be part of some unsa-
vory business on purpose, but how was he to know the depth
of her character from such a short acquaintance?

At first, when Amanda tried to question him, he told her he wanted to get away from Lindquist as quickly and quietly as possible. They rode on for several hours in silence, Cal wanting to get to Bozeman soon. It had been over a month since he'd been to a town, and the last visit had been brief at best. He knew of Ned Bart, but it seemed like that guy had stepped it up a notch.

Amanda rode behind him as usual. Though her arms still rested around his body, Cal did not feel the same intimacy of the night before; it was clear she was wrapped up in thoughts and was far away from him. He missed that feeling.

"Cal," said Amanda, breaking the silence. "He said my brother wasn't in a position to send anyone to look for his sister. What does that mean? Do you think he's dead?"

Cal could hear the anxiety in her voice.

"No. At least, that fellow didn't think so. Sounds like your stepbrother is in hiding."

"Oh," she said. After a long pause, she added, "Why?"

Cal didn't have a good answer for that. Instead, he said, "Amanda, tell me about your stepbrother."

"Well, I... He..." Cal thought she seemed to struggle momentarily, to summarize a brother she was suddenly confused about—or to make up a story? Cal wasn't sure which it was. But she spoke anyway.

"He's five years older than I am. My father married Samuel's mother when I was ten. Samuel's my stepbrother, you see? He only lived on the farm about two years, then he apprenticed out to a storekeeper in the next town over and lived with the storekeeper's family. My mother's sister's husband's brother, that is." She paused as though waiting for Cal to process the family connection. He nodded.

"And he lived and worked there until he was twenty-three," she finished off.

"You were close?"

"No, not terribly. He came home for holidays, and some days off, but I didn't see him too much. But it was almost always great fun when he did come, bringing penny candy or ribbons to give out. He told the funniest stories about the customers he served."

Even though Amanda was behind him, Cal could imagine the smile on her face as she reminisced. She seemed to have a fondness for her stepbrother.

"Almost always fun?"

"Well, yes. A few times, when he came home, he was upset with the storekeeper. He would expect our parents to take his side, and his mother did. But my father would remind Samuel he was an apprentice and ought to be quiet and learn. Samuel didn't like that."

When she trailed off into her memories, Cal pushed for more. "How did he come to Montana Territory?"

Amanda's voice turned wistful. "He read about it like we all did. The West. Being a young man, he could act on it. It was an easy choice after he and the storekeeper had a falling out. Samuel was courting the storekeeper's daughter secretly, you see."

"That doesn't seem right," said Cal.

"Samuel said he loved her, but her father thought she was too young and Samuel could wait. He got so mad he up and quit, Samuel told me.

"So, he came and asked my father for a loan, then packed up and headed west. He mined briefly and got a small hit. Enough to set himself up as a storekeeper in Virginia City. He mentioned in a letter how he was thinking of bringing in an assistant. You know the rest."

Cal was still in the dark. Amanda clearly thought her stepbrother was a decent man, but Cal was beginning to question that assumption. "What else can you tell me about your step-brother?"

He heard Miss Amanda make a deep sigh and wasn't sure if she was just struggling to come up with more or exasperated at his questioning. No matter; it was important to find out as much as possible.

"Samuel Emerson. Brown hair. Brown eyes. He's always been called Big Em, on account of his tall stature."

Whoa! That changed things. Cal had heard Amanda mention her brother Samuel. A common enough name. But Big Em, yes, he knew of him. A tall, skinny man from back East who'd struck it rich, opened a bar, gambled away his proceeds, stiffed some tradesmen, and gotten into a lot of drunken brawls. All in a very short time.

"Amanda, I don't think your brother's letters were entirely truthful. He did open a business, a bar if I recall, but it closed down… maybe eight months ago."

Cal didn't think Amanda realized she was wringing her hands together.

"You must be mistaken. His last letter was sent two months ago. Maybe you are mistaking Samuel for another."

"Well, I don't go into towns much lately. Things may have changed. But I don't think there are two tall, gangly men from back East called Big Em."

He was twisted in the saddle, trying to look at Amanda directly. He could see the struggle in her eyes. She wanted him to be wrong about her brother, but she could see the truth in his words. Or at least, she saw that he had no reason to lie to her about this.

"Could he be mining again? Maybe that's where the money came from."

"Sure could." Cal doubted it, but he so wanted to assuage Amanda's concern. He couldn't see a reason for Samuel Emerson to lie to the family about the source of his income in such a case, but lots of men wanted to prove their success on their own terms, even if it was invented. And lots of men wrote letters home that weren't entirely truthful.

"But why is he in trouble with this Ned Bart?"

"That I can't say," said Cal. "But maybe, when we get to town, we can figure this out."

Amanda put her hand onto Cal's wrist. She looked forlorn. "What is he doing? What am I doing?"

Cal didn't know what to say, except he knew he wanted to keep Amanda safe. He didn't like seeing her scared, either for her person or for her future. He put his hand over hers.

"It'll be alright, Amanda. We'll figure it out."

He turned to face forward again. Even though he wasn't twisted in the saddle to see Amanda's face, he could feel the tension in the muscles of her arms wrapped around him. He held his hand over hers tighter and started the horse trotting. The bumpy ride would get them to their next destination a little faster and, perhaps, distract her from her anxious thoughts.

On the crest of the trail, they paused. Cal turned his horse so Amanda could look to the side to see the view, and not have to peer over his shoulder.

Before them, the mountains opened up into a beautiful valley, green and tan and brown. Across the open land she saw another range of mountains, purple-grey in the distance. Above it all stretched a bluebird sky.

"Oh," breathed Amanda.

Cal smiled. He could tell from her awed tone and tighter grip around his waist that she saw the same majesty he saw. She brushed against him as she turned to take in all aspects of the valley.

"I can see why everyone is moving here."

"Actually, most folks are crossing the Madison," he pointed

toward a mountain range, "over there, to where the gold is. But some of us, we see the chance for farming here."

"You, too?"

Once again, talking with Amanda while they were on horseback was allowing one of them to open up. This time, it was him.

"I've claimed some land a little northwest of Bozeman. A brand-new town, small, but growing. That's where we're headed now after you've had your fill of the view."

"I thought we were going to Virginia City."

"We need supplies. And, we need to find out what's going on. About your brother... and you."

Cal pulled on the reins to halt Miss Molly. "Here, let me show you."

He dismounted and turned immediately to help Amanda down. He led her around the horse's head to a flat spot of dirt on the trail. He reached to the side of the trail and came back with a stick. He began to draw...

First, some triangles for the mountains where they currently stood. Then a small circle to the left of them. "That's Bozeman." A dot a little northwest of it. "That's my home-stead," he said. Farther to the left, he drew a middle-sized circle. "That's Gallatin City." Below that, he created a big circle. "That's Virginia City." Then he pointed across the valley. "Across those mountains."

Amanda nodded her understanding.

"I think we should go into Bozeman and see what we can learn," Cal said. "From there, we'll know whether to head to Virginia City directly or not."

"And what if it's *not?*" She looked out across the valley.

"We'll have to see. One option is to catch the ferry across the Missouri near Gallatin City. You can head up to Fort Benton, catch a steamboat back East." She looked startled to hear that. He knew she didn't know how bad it could get if

Bart had it out for her. He didn't want to think about it himself. He liked to think he could keep her safe, but considering what they were to each other—which was not much at this point—how could he claim such a thing?

There was another pause and then Amanda's quiet voice came. "I'm feeling awfully scared right now." Her head was bowed and her eyes were closed, perhaps to hold in tears.

Cal patted her hand. Maybe it was more of a caress, he suspected. But she didn't pull away, so he continued.

"Then why don't you stay my fiancée?" It felt strangely good to say those words. "You know, just a little longer. Until we find out what's going on. That'll help keep your true identity from Ned Bart and his men."

It all made sense to him, until Amanda said, "What about your real fiancée?" and gently pulled her hand from under his.

What about her? What could he say? That he had made a plan and now he wasn't sure it was a good one? That he might not honor his word to another lady? He tried to explain.

"My father wrote to me earlier this year. A childhood friend of mine had been widowed and was looking to start over. She was having trouble moving on because of her husband's family. They're wealthy and important in town and don't want to believe their son was killed in the war.

"So, with the help of my father, we agreed to a tentative engagement—so that she could travel with less hassle."

Amanda looked at him skeptically.

"I haven't seen her, or exchanged letters, or anything since I left Missouri. I have fond memories of the girl. But I don't know the woman," Cal tried to justify the situation. "And she doesn't know me."

"Plus, she's supervising the transport of some mining equipment for my partner and myself," he added. After all, who could Amanda tell?

Her eyebrows rose even further.

"If folks think she's bringing homesteading supplies instead of mining equipment, well, it's better for us that they don't know what's going on. There are problems with claim jumpers and outright robbers."

Amanda's brows returned to normal and she gave a short nod.

"So you're a miner, too?"

"Yes."

Amanda was looking out at the valley and mountains. Cal wasn't sure what he wanted her to say. He added, "The last letter from my father said she was preparing to leave this past spring. I didn't know when she'd arrive." He looked at the dirt-encrusted creases of his hands. "I sure didn't know she *had* arrived."

He didn't like that Delia had arrived and he wasn't there to greet her and make sure she was safe. He also didn't like that Ollie Linquist knew it all before he did.

Amanda looked up from Cal's dirt map. "We ought to move along."

Cal turned and gathered the horses. He mounted Miss Molly and pulled Amanda up behind him again. She rested her forehead against his back.

Cal couldn't help but reconsider his plan. It had all seemed rather clever at first. His childhood friend could justify leaving her hometown and heading west if she had a fiancé to meet her. He could ensure his expensive equipment was chaperoned in transport. Seemed easy. Seemed sensible. Then.

And, Cal admitted to himself, he had even wondered if, upon re-acquaintance, they would find themselves willing to make the engagement a real one. He had a homestead and he liked the idea of a family at this time in his life. Not having seen Delia in so long, though, he had only one face to put on the wife of that imaginary family; it was Amanda's face.

Cal shook his head and then clucked to the horses. The two

animals, packing people on one and packs on the other, picked up their pace heading out of the mountains. Ears tipped forward, they were heading toward rest and grain.

Moments later, Cal heard Amanda's ragged intake of breath and realized she was crying.

CHAPTER 11

Amanda sat on a boulder overlooking the Gallatin Valley. It was beautiful. Mountains surrounded the broad expanse in every direction. She could see the evergreen trees crowding up the mountains, their dark green foliage only thinning out at the higher elevations where rocky outcrops and grassy peaks invited her. In the distance, the farther mountain ranges were grey, sharp and smudged with the haze of a hot day.

And the valley...

It was broad and flat and unburdened by factories and workhouses and slums. It was green and brown and spoke of a host of dreams.

She looked at the beautiful country and her eyes welled with tears again. She lifted her arm to wipe them away on her sleeve. She'd started crying while riding behind Cal on Miss Molly. She'd been embarrassed, but unable to stop herself. Between sobs, she'd managed to mumble, "Please, I need a moment." Cal had halted the horse immediately. She slid off without waiting for help and ran to an outcropping of rocks, sliding down behind it to sit with her knees up, a cradle in which to hide her tears.

That moment had lasted thirty minutes, she guessed. Her eyes hurt from crying. She felt like a wet dishrag.

"Amanda?"

And there was Cal. He had an uncanny ability to read her. He seemed to read the wilderness and the animals so well, so why not her, too?

"Do you want to talk?"

That simple question. It reminded her of how different the response would have been from her dear friends back at the boarding house. "Amanda, what's wrong?!" A hug and refusal to be put off. Friends who knew her and wanted to know, wanted to help. Someone would grab her hands and pull her to the sofa, or the side of a bed. A huddle of comfort.

"I—" she choked. She wanted to say no. She wanted to say yes. She felt the tears welling up in her eyes again, more tears, spilling over. She buried her face in her hands.

Cal's hand rested softly on her shoulder, patting her occasionally. This should not have mattered, but it did. Her sobs came harder. It was not at all the way she wanted to be seen by Cal, or by any man, but it didn't matter.

The emotions inside of her would not be dammed.

At last, she calmed. Her shoulders stopped shaking and she managed to pull her kerchief from her pocket to wipe her eyes, cheeks, and nose.

She said, "I'm sorry," and glanced up at Cal, who was sitting on the rock above her, his hand still on her shoulder. She expected him to look stoic, as her father might have, or terribly uncomfortable, as her brothers might have. Cal, however, looked concerned. Genuinely concerned.

She gave a short laugh. "I seem to have a surplus of emotions right now."

She expected Cal to bolt. Who could blame him? Instead,

he took his hand off her shoulder and slid down the rock to sit beside her, hips and shoulders touching. He looked at her face intently, and then out at the view.

"It's a lot to take in, isn't it?" he said.

Amanda knew he wasn't speaking of the view only.

He continued. "I came out here nearly ten years ago. My uncle got work on an exploratory expedition and invited me to come along. I was twenty years old. I've been exploring, tracking, trapping, mining ever since... Back home, I was brought up to be a farmer. My father had plans to divide up his land among his sons and to marry the daughters into getting some other land. He studied the land, and the markets, and told everyone what to plant, and when, who to marry, and when. It was a good, solid life, surrounded by family."

"But not the life you wanted?" Amanda offered. She leaned infinitesimally into his shoulder. She looked ahead, but out the corner of her eye, she saw him glance down at her.

"That's right. Maybe, if it could have started later in life, I'd have found it satisfactory. Maybe if I'd had my eye on a particular girl it would have seemed more appealing. But I was young for my age. Where some saw a potential bride, I saw a playmate."

He shrugged. "Sometimes, when it's particularly rough out here, I wonder where I'd be if I'd stayed. Married, likely. Children? Would I be content, or pulling on the bit of my father's reins? Maybe, if I hadn't experienced all this, maybe I could have done it. I was longing for something different, though."

"Did you find it?" She looked at him now, wanting to know.

"Yes. No... and yes." He looked right back at her, deep into her eyes, and she felt a rightness, a completeness. She tried to remember how long she had known him. And that there was another woman out there, planning—or at least hoping—to marry him.

A woman wouldn't travel across the country into the wilds of Montana Territory if she thought her fiancé might take one look at her and say, "Nah, I don't think we suit." Amanda was glad Cal couldn't read her mind.

Cal's mouth crooked up in a smile. "Are you afraid you won't find what you are looking for?"

She smiled back. "Yes and no. I can see the glory of this land, why people want to come here." She swept her arm out as though to embrace the land before her. "It's just so different. Wild country, not the city. I worked in a mill. Six days a week of sameness. Not even the seasonal changes of farming that I grew up with. Women, everywhere women in the factories, except the foreman. A woman's boarding house with a widow-woman in charge. Go to the market and the stores for supplies. A visit to my father every few months. I wanted a change, and a chance to make something of my life, but this is... so very different.

"Here, it's men, and wild things and every day is different. No store, no market. I don't even sleep in the same place each night."

"That will change," said Cal. He looked out over the land. "This valley is already changing, with more and more folks coming to stay."

"It's not just that. Everything has been going wrong. From leaving the mill to leaving the wagon train, to leaving Smitty's mule train." Amanda realized she was speaking rapidly and had turned to face Cal directly. She could not slow down. Like the tears before, the words were unstoppable. "Strange men hunting me. My stepbrother—what is going on with him? I made plans, however misguidedly, that revolved around my brother and his store. But there may not even be a store, and now it seems he is in trouble regardless. And I am in trouble by association."

Cal put a finger up to her lips. She took a deep breath and tried to steady her emotions.

"Let's think about this," he said. "You left the mill because...?"

"I got labeled a rabble-rouser for trying to improve the working conditions."

"You left the wagon train because...?"

"Geraldine's widower thought I would step in as the replacement wife." She gave a shudder. "One of the other men on the wagon train found Pastor Frank—we were at Fort Laramie—and asked him to say the service for Geraldine and her babies. We got to talking and I asked the pastor for help getting to Virginia City. When he heard my story, he was eager to help and brought me over to Smitty."

"Of course he was," muttered Cal.

"What's that supposed to mean?"

"Come on, Amanda. You're a beautiful young woman. Even pastors want to marry. Especially pastors. He would have followed you when we left Smitty if I'd allowed it."

Amanda had to think about how she felt. She was flattered that Cal thought she was beautiful but resentful of the impression it was somehow her fault Pastor Frank befriended her. Or that he'd perhaps wanted more.

Once again, she wished she had her women friends to lean on. She had a flash of insight that life here would never be—no, could never be—the same. Not only jobs and the day to day work of living, or the lack of a market like she'd just been talking about. But simply because of the male-dominated culture and the lack of women friends she would find. She'd known this in her mind but was only now realizing it in her heart.

Cal was certainly different from her friends back home, she thought, looking at his scruffy beard. But perhaps it wasn't all bad.

"I realize that I will get a life very different from my old one if I want to stay. And that there is no way I could truly know what life will be like here. I have started a train with no brakes. I must be insane."

"Do you need brakes?"

Amanda paused to sort out the feelings roiling inside of her breast. "I am scared. I am excited."

Cal gave her a wry smile that she could not help but answer in kind. "I declare you sane."

She laughed. He slapped his thigh with his hat. "Now, let's ride out."

CHAPTER 12

Cal wound the pack line along the deer path, heading not for Bozeman but for a homestead along a gentle creek descending out of a spring in the foothills of the Bridger Mountains. He knew Amanda was anxious to find her stepbrother, that she didn't need to see this place, and that it was more important to him that she see it. But, he had another, more valid excuse.

He could feel Amanda twisting around behind him.

"Do you need a break," he asked.

"No-o-o," came her reply, "but I'm confused. Are we heading into the town? I thought it was in that direction." She pointed out to their side, toward the setting sun. They'd reviewed that rough map, drawn in the dirt, earlier in the day. She clearly was trying to get the lay of the land. He admired her attitude; this was a woman who took life by the horns, despite the misgivings she'd voiced earlier.

"It's farther south than that," he said, pointing back over his shoulder. "It took us a little longer to get here than I'd planned. I'd rather not show up in town just before dark. We don't know if your friends are waiting for you."

"Not my friends," he heard her mumble.

"We'll spend the night out by Spring Creek, get cleaned up, and head into town in the morning. That way, I can scope it out with my looking glass before we're in the middle of it." The day had warmed up considerably, and he looked forward washing off the sweat and dust he'd accumulated.

The horses and mules weaved among the red branches and green leaves of the willows. The air was sweeter and fresher, and the animals, knowing they were near rest and shade, picked up their pace.

"Is that going to work? We could spend all day circling the town, looking along the edges for the men whose faces we wouldn't know anyway."

Cal laughed. "And just how big do you think this town is?"

He felt Amanda swat his shoulder. "Why are you laughing? What don't I know?"

"Bozeman was only incorporated last August. It's platted and all, but there are only... let me remember... ten buildings, maybe a few more since my last visit. It really was just a crossing place until last year—called Jacob's Crossing. And mostly still is, though John Bozeman and the others are hoping for more."

"This John Bozeman must be important if they named the town after him." She sounded impressed.

Cal didn't like that. John was a smooth-talking charmer who liked pretty ladies. "Don't go thinking that."

"Will there be a place for me to stay?"

"Oh, there's a hotel. Big enough for the owner to get married in last winter. Big enough, too, for women and children to hide in earlier this summer when folks thought the Sioux were going to raid."

Cal heard Amanda's intake of breath. Maybe he shouldn't have mentioned that last. But then, maybe it was good for her to be reminded of the risks of living out in Montana Territory.

Just then, the willow bushes opened up onto a creek and an open field.

One side drifted back up into the foothills. The other opened up for a jaw-dropping view of the valley. The land was green and brown, the horizon just turning golden with purple streaks among the clouds.

"Oh my," Amanda whispered, and this time Cal was pleased with the awe in her voice. They splashed across the stream and then walked up the hill to a flattened spot. It was his favorite place.

The creek flowed behind them, the mountains to the north, and the valley opening up to the west. It was breathtaking. Knowing she would get a break there, a chance to clean up and feel respectable again made it even more appealing. Amanda noticed a fire pit just as Cal swung off the horse. He turned to help her dismount, his hands grasping her around the waist.

Amanda said, "What a lovely spot. Do you stop here often?"

He looked at her without removing his hands. "Whenever I can. I've filed a claim and I've started improving it."

"Oh," she said, now feeling utterly confused. Who was this mountain man really? "So, you don't want to be a mountain man anymore?"

Cal laughed and lifted her by the waist to spin her around. He dropped his hands and moved to stand beside her. He placed his right arm across her upper back, grasping her far shoulder to steer her into position. "See that stand of trees way yonder?" She nodded. He swung her around to face west. "See that dip over there, with the blue flowers diving into it?" She nodded, and he swung her again. "Now, see those cottonwoods there?" She nodded at the sight of the big, gnarled trees. "This is all mine. I've claimed it." At this he threw out his other arm and spun them in a circle, "And I'm homesteading it. I'm going to call it...well, I don't know. It's my paradise is all I know."

His smile was beautiful and infectious. Amanda laughed at his joy, and at her own misjudgment of him. It was confusing to know so little of a person and yet to put her life in his hands. And to do it so... comfortably. She withdrew from his embrace. "It's a wonderful place, Cal."

She spun around, trying to take it all in. "What happened over there?" She pointed to a blackened tree trunk down the creek a little way. It looked to be a large cottonwood with a Y-split in its trunk.

"Lightning strikes last summer."

Amanda grabbed his wrist. "Is that common?" She didn't like lightning storms.

"We get our share," Cal said, eyeing her concern. "But don't worry too much. Lightning doesn't usually strike twice."

"Usually?"

"That tree is unusual. One strike hit that side of the tree over there," he pointed. "It caused a little fire, but the rain doused it. A week later, another storm brought another strike to the other side. It smoldered a couple of days, but luckily didn't spread."

Amanda found herself unable to look away. Once again, the world out West was turning out to be bigger—and badder—than she had dreamed.

"There's more." Cal turned Amanda away from the tree and led her toward a rise. He stepped around a large sagebrush, and there was a door in the hillside. She looked more carefully and saw a small window, largely covered over with dry grasses. He pushed open the door, and she could see he'd have to duck to enter.

It was dark inside, the only light coming from the open doorway. She saw a wooden shutter blocking the small window she'd seen from the outside. The walls and floor, and—she looked up—even its ceiling were all dirt.

There was a small table with a hurricane lamp and a plate, bowl, and cup stacked together on it. Then, she saw a low bedstand with a thin mattress over the ropes. There was a single beam running across the ceiling and from it hung a pot, a serving fork and spoon, and a burlap bag. A three-legged stool sat stacked with newspapers.

She poked the burlap bag. It didn't swing much, laden down with weight.

"Food staples, hung to try to keep the critters out," Cal offered.

Amanda pointed to the stack of newspapers. "You must like to read. Is that the Bozeman paper?"

Cal smiled. "I do. It can get lonely out here and it's a way to stay in touch with the rest of the world. There's no Bozeman paper yet, though; I get one from Virginia City when I can. I'm collecting them, too."

His voice took on an excited quality.

"I've been gathering materials, like these newspapers for insulation. Next month, I plan to start building a proper cabin. My friend J.B. will come over from Virginia City to help build. It'll have two rooms. One for the kitchen and sitting, one for the family to sleep in, someday. Up until recently, I was part here, part mountains, and part Virginia City. I thought it best to keep it all less noticeable so I don't find my possessions disappearing," he said.

The word *family* stuck in Amanda's head. She thought of the fiancée steaming upriver to meet her childhood friend-turned-mountain-man-turned-homesteader. She imagined starting a new life with this handsome and capable man in this most sublime place.

Amanda had been looking forward to a new, independent life in Virginia City with her brother. And she acknowledged to herself that she'd hoped she might meet a decent man to love and marry, to have a family with and to grow old with. She'd wanted these things in the abstract, but now, in this place, she could really see it, taste it. It wasn't just her imagination or dreams; it felt tangible and real.

And that was because of Cal.

Amanda's heart swelled even as her dreams dimmed. She could not wish in her mind for something other than what was in front of her. And she could not have what was there in front of her; Cal had a fiancée already.

Not only that, but he had a fiancée who was a wealthy widow. Cal was so proud and Amanda worried how a woman accustomed to finer things might perceive this dugout.

"Are you sure your fiancée will want to live here?"

"What?" Cal drew back.

Oh dear, she thought. *That didn't come out the way I intended.*

"Is there a well? Have you built an outhouse? Your fiancée will probably want an outhouse this winter."

She put on a smile and looked over his shoulder, not quite meeting his eyes. She shaded her face as though the light coming in the doorway was too bright. She was surprised to find that encouraging him to make it more appealing for his fiancée made her feel bad for herself.

Amanda stepped around Cal but stopped in the doorway. Just then, the bright sun dropped under the horizon. There was still plenty of light in the sky.

"Will you show me where you will build the cabin? Right here?"

Cal just looked at her for a moment. She could tell she'd offended him, but he was too proud of his homestead to hold a grudge.

"I'll show you."

He led her behind the dugout, talking about the root cellar he'd already dug, the field he was clearing, and the crop he wanted to plant. Cal still looked like a mountain man, thought Amanda, but now he talked like a farmer.

Well, if he could reinvent himself, so could she. She'd find a way to start her new life in Virginia City, with our without her stepbrother's help.

CHAPTER 13

"Oh my," said Amanda.

Cal looked up from the campfire he was tending. The coffee was boiling and the bacon was sizzling, but it was nothing compared to the look on Amanda's face. She had halted halfway between the dugout, where she'd spent the night, and the fire. She was staring at Cal. He had gotten up early to bath in the creek and shave. He had put aside his mountain leathers for his town clothes. His denim pants and plaid cotton shirt were crisp and clean, and he knew he looked a far cry from how he'd appeared the past few days.

And Amanda? She seemed to like it. He gave her a wide smile. That startled her out of her stare. Her face turned red and she focused on smoothing out the fabric at the waist of her dress.

"I'm sorry I'm so late. It's been so long since I slept indoors... I was very comfortable. I felt safe." She glanced over at his bedroll, still laid out on the ground where he'd slept. "Thank you for giving up your bed."

"I was glad to do it," Cal said. "Coffee?"

They left after breakfast for the short ride into town. Cal

paused when they were a distance from the small cluster of buildings. He took out his binoculars and scanned the area. Satisfied, he placed them back into their leather carrier.

"Everything looks normal in Jacob's Cross—" He corrected himself. "In Bozeman, I mean." He was pretty sure some of his disgust at the name, or at least, the namesake, was apparent, but Amanda didn't seem to notice. "I even see Smitty's mules."

"This is 'town,' then, is it?" she asked.

"What? Too small for you?"

"No, it's just, I've heard," she turned to look at him and, with his head turned, their faces were close together. She paused and started again. "I'd heard that thousands of men were pouring into the territory. I thought there'd be more to it. That's all."

He wanted to kiss her, he realized, looking at her lips so close to his own. He wanted to kiss her. A lot.

He pulled his head around and made a show of clucking his horses into position. Once he'd dropped off his supplies in town, he'd have no excuse to have Amanda keep sharing his horse. He was disappointed. As the horses started walking, he responded.

"They're pouring in, but mostly to the mining towns. This isn't a mining town. It'll be a mining support town, and a rancher and farmer support town. I have high hopes for the area, and so do the founders."

Cal found the growth and progress of Montana Territory exciting. With hard work and a smart head on his shoulders, men like him had unlimited opportunities there. The progress was exciting, usually; each visit into town, any town, brought new faces and new buildings with new businesses. But sometimes, well, sometimes he missed the natural order of the wilderness. Nothing seemed... nonsensical there, the way it sometimes did when people were involved. That's why he was still part fur-trapper, part-miner, part-homesteader. He wanted only so much time spent around other people.

He wondered if Amanda could be the exception.

At this moment, though, he was more than willing to go into *town*... to see if he could find out what was going on with Amanda's brother. And to know there were some good, sensible men he could depend on and not be at the mercy of an ambush again, out in the wilderness.

He steered Miss Molly and the trailing horse to a corral. He removed their ropes and put them inside. He and Amanda walked across the street to the hotel, though he was quite certain it also wouldn't qualify as one by Amanda's Eastern standards. But there were rooms for rent and that was sufficient.

He helped Amanda to get a room and arrange for a hot bath. At the door to the room, as he handed her satchels over, she said, "I'm looking forward to some time to myself. And I'm sure you're glad to be rid of me for a while."

And she closed the door in his face.

Ouch, thought Cal.

Cal hadn't really wanted to leave her, even for a moment, but he didn't want her spending any more time out in the open than necessary until they had figured out what was going on, and how to fix it. And it was best, he told himself, not to get too caught up in her situation anyhow. They'd probably figure out this was a case of mistaken identity and all would be well. She'd go work with her brother, at least until someone swept her off her feet. And it probably wouldn't be a man who'd spent the last decade in the company of bears more than people, and one who was foolish enough to show her the dugout cabin she'd have to live in. The one that didn't even have an outhouse. Yet.

He stomped down the stairs to the small bar set up in the dining room. Rob was still there, ostensibly polishing a glass while waiting for Cal. The slender, rope-muscled man was permanently tanned and permanently creased from a lifetime spent outdoors. His hotel and livery were concessions to his age and increasingly creaky bones. Cal liked him, and more importantly for today, trusted him.

"Rumor Rob! Good to see you."

"And you, Cal. Usual?" He slid a small glass of amber whiskey across the bar top.

"Thanks." He started to swig it as Rob settled into his *let's have a chat* pose, both elbows propped on the bar.

"So, your fiancée upstairs... is she... is she the same one that was waiting on you in Gallatin City? Because I heard that one's a brunette."

Cal choked on his drink. He'd been hoping to postpone dealing with that situation a little longer. "No, and you're going to have to keep that quiet."

He explained the situation with the hairy mountain man threats. Rob's face changed from eager gossiper to concerned citizen.

"I've got to keep them confused until I work this out. What do you know about Samuel Emerson?" At Rob's quizzical expression, Cal added, "Big Em."

Rob's expression slipped past concerned to fearful. "Ohhh, your girl's in a heap of trouble."

Cal's heart sank.

"Samuel was a barkeeper in Virginia City for about a day and a half, but he had the gambling bug and lost it quick. He started hiring out to shakedown miners. From there, he fell into Ned Bart's posse. Then, things escalated." Rob leaned in and lowered his voice. "They say he was Ned's right-hand man before things went sour." He glanced around before adding, "Before the Parker shootout."

Cal leaned in and lowered his own voice to match. "Bob, I've been out of town for a bit. I haven't heard about that."

Despite his concern for talking about the criminal element, Cal could see Rob was pleased to have fresh ears for his story. There was a reason the fellow's nickname was *Rumor*. He waved his glass in front of Rob's eyes to get a refill before the storytelling commenced.

"Rumor had it that John Parker struck gold at his mine—big gold, I'm telling you—and was hiding it at his homestead. Ned led a group of his men to Parker's place outside Virginia City. Parker, turns out, had hired a few fellows as guard. You know, last year's Innocents were mostly caught and hung, but those robberies and killings are still fresh in everyone's minds." He nodded at Cal for agreement, and so Cal nodded back. It was true. "So, the two groups met and there was a shootout. Somehow, Big Em shot Billy Tremble."

"Who?"

Rob pulled back. "You been living under a rock, Cal?"

Cal took a deep breath. "I told you; I've been out of circulation for a bit. Now hurry up and fill me in."

Rob gave a look of exasperated disappointment that reminded Cal of his old schoolteacher.

"Billy—he's Ned's cousin. A young fellow. He showed up a few months back, and rumor has it he was trying to push Big Em out. Blood is thicker than water, and all that."

"So Samuel shot him on purpose," Cal asked.

"Big Em killed him on purpose," Rob whispered, emphasis on the *killed*. "That's what Ned Bart thinks anyway. He's gunning for Big Em, has all his men gunning for Big Em, and rumor says Big Em is hit and dying."

Rob grabbed another glass to wipe. Cal tried to wrap his mind around this man Big Em, a far cry from the man Amanda thought she knew.

"But why's he after Samuel's sister, then?"

"Ned is making an example of Samuel. An eye for an eye. A sister for a cousin."

Cal gripped the edge of the bar with both hands. "This guy's an animal! Where's the law?"

"Well, you're not wrong. The law's been tightening things up in Virginia City and the other mining towns, the ones that have law nearby that is, so Ned's rumored to be avoiding those areas and staying in the wilds. He strikes like a rattlesnake and then disappears back under his rock. So rumor has it."

Cal turned around to look out the door. It was bright outside, a stark contrast to the dim room. What was he going to do? He had Amanda's stories about Samuel, and he had Rob's stories about Samuel. None of this told him how to help her.

"What else is happening?"

"Smitty arrived yesterday. They set up camp south of town, except Richard. He's staying with the Beals so Mrs. Beal can attend to his shot leg. Smitty told about that gunfight. He's got a preacher with him. That fellow's wandering around looking for a flock. I told him to keep looking… in Virginia City." Rob laughed at his own joke. "And they were all asking if I'd seen you and this young woman, though they weren't calling her your fiancée." Rob gave a sly smile. "And, as I mentioned, rumor has it there's a pretty young woman in Gallatin City who says she's your fiancée, too."

Cal wished he could back up a couple of days, to when he had no fiancées and life was a great deal simpler.

Cal waved his glass at the barkeep. He'd have one more drink before he had to go tell Amanda how dire the situation was.

CHAPTER 14

C al knocked on the door to Amanda's room. She asked, "Who is it?" before opening it and giving him a sweet smile. Her hair was still wet, smooth against her head and tied in a loose braid in the back. She wore a dress he hadn't seen yet, a fresh and clean light green with little yellow flowers dotted all over it. Nothing about her situation had changed, but she looked happier.

"That must have been quite a bath. You look like a new person."

Amanda blushed, her hand resting against the doorframe. "I feel like a new person. You should try it."

"Well, I don't know if I should be offended by that."

"That's not what I meant!"

He laughed and, after an awkward moment, she laughed with him.

"Did you find any information? Do you know what's going on with Samuel?"

"I have some information. If you're not uncomfortable, I could come in there so we can speak privately."

Amanda nodded her head and then stepped back to let Cal

into the room. They sat on the edge of her bed. He rested his forearms on his thighs, staring at the floor. He did not want to be the bearer of this bad news.

"Cal?" She lightly touched his arm for an instant.

He turned to look her in the eyes.

"Samuel is not who you thought he was." He proceeded to share what he had learned, from Samuel's business failure to his descent into a life of crime, from a swaggering outlaw to an injured, dying man hiding in the wilds. "After he shot Ned's cousin, accidental or not, he knew Ned wouldn't forget it. So he snatched several bags of gold and took off."

"Is that when he got shot?"

"I believe so, though the story is a little unclear. All I know is he's badly hurt and in hiding, because Ned wants his gold and his revenge."

He watched as the new light shining out of Amanda dimmed. Her shoulders slumped and he only wished he could make her feel better.

"He might be, he… I'm not… What should… I don't know…" she said.

Cal leaned back and over to wrap his arm around Amanda's shoulders.

"You're not alone. I'll help you figure this out."

She tipped her head into his shoulder, eyes glassy with barely-restrained tears. "Thank you, Cal. You are… thank you."

He decided to address the question that had been nagging him. "Unfortunately, Ned's revenge includes you. I'd sure like to know how they found you on the Bozeman Trail."

Amanda shrugged. "I'm not sure, but I may be at fault. I wrote a letter to Samuel and posted it from Fort Laramie, telling him about my change in plans."

Cal patted her arm, a *there there* gesture. "When did you send it?"

"Only the day before we left. There were ten days from Geraldine's death until Smitty was ready to travel. The soldiers wouldn't let us leave until they knew there weren't too many Sioux nearby. It made me nervous, so I decided at the last moment to write... in case I was killed by Indians along the way. I wanted someone to know what happened to me," Amanda said. She looked at Cal with her damp eyes. He hated the thought that her life could have been snuffed out before he'd ever met her.

They sat in silence for a few moments. Cal was bothered by the question still. "I don't see how that letter could have beat you to the area. The Bozeman Trail is the newest, shortest route. And there are no telegraphs in the area. But perhaps if someone had sent a letter not long after Geraldine's death, as soon as you made the decision... perhaps it could have made it in time."

Time was hanging over Cal's head. How did Ned's men find Amanda on the trail without time for sending messages? How much time would pass until they found her again? And besides Amanda and her troubles, Cal had his own ticking clock. He knew he couldn't leave Delia waiting for him indefinitely.

He leaned slightly into Amanda's shoulder.

"I have to go to Gallatin City. It's the closest big town before Virginia City and since rumor has it Ned's been hanging out in the valley, it's the place most likely to have information about him or Samuel... Plus," he took a deep breath, "there's a woman there asking for me and I need to take care of that situation."

He felt Amanda stiffen. "Your fiancée?"

"Yes."

"When do we leave?"

"I think you'll be safer here. Fewer people to see you. Plus, if Ned thinks there's only one fiancée, he'll be less likely to suspect you're really Samuel's sister than if he realizes there's another gal over in Gallatin City claiming that title."

Amanda pulled away from him and raised an eyebrow. "Claiming the title, eh?"

Now he repeated her words back to her: "I didn't mean it that way!"

They both laughed. It was the sad laughter of desperation, but it helped to cut the tension anyway. Cal stood up to leave, but first, he had something to ask Amanda.

"I've asked Rumor Rob to make us up a supper if you're interested. We can eat down in the parlor." Her face stilled, and Cal didn't know if she liked his idea. He added in a scramble, "If you don't want to, I can have your supper brought up here. For you. Not me." He twisted the brim of his hat and wished he was standing somewhere else.

Amanda smiled and Cal felt the tension leaving his hands. She dipped her head as she said, "No. I mean... I'd like that."

He took two big steps to the door and opened it for her. He held it wide as she walked by him, the bottom of her skirt brushing the tops of his boots. In the hall, he offered his arm, which she took, and together they walked downstairs.

In the dining parlor, which was also the bar, hotel reception and the best place to arrange for any livery services, there was a table set for two. Cal had asked Rob to put them away from the window and door; it made Cal feel a little safer knowing he could spot someone coming in. He didn't normally carry his gun to dinner, but given the circumstances, felt it necessary.

Away from the sunlight that filtered in, it was dim, and feeling a bit intimate. Cal felt like he was courting Amanda, and told himself that since they were claiming to be engaged, it was the right thing to do. *Act normal...* even though he was technically—sort of—engaged to another woman. He didn't want to think about that.

He slid the wooden chair out from the edge of the table.

Amanda sat down in the chair, looking so calm and lady-like. Her blond hair was lightening as it dried and framed her sun-pinked face and blue eyes. He couldn't help being in awe of her.

"I can hardly believe," he said, "that you were shot in the side just the other day. You look like a fancy lady."

Amanda blushed and smiled reluctantly.

"That's a compliment, you know," he said.

She smiled again. "I know. It's just… well, it's not one I ever expected to receive: *You look pretty good for having been shot.*"

He laughed and then sobered. "In fact, I think you look lovely, regardless of whether you've been shot." He reached out and put his hand on hers. "Is that any better? I admire your fortitude and bravery, and particularly like how they're wrapped up in such a pretty package."

He loved watching her blush. It made her eyes seem a little bluer even.

"You don't look like a mountain man anymore," Amanda said. He noticed she was redirecting the conversation but had left her hand resting under his.

"You noticed?" He waggled his eyebrows at her and realized he couldn't stop himself from flirting. "Have you been watching me, Miss Amanda?"

She was saved from answering his teasing question by the arrival of their food. They pulled their hands apart as Rob placed a bowl of deer stew in front of each of them.

"Will you still… be a mountain man? You know, now that you're homesteading?" Amanda asked as she picked up a spoon.

"I'm not a mountain man, not really. I trap some in the winter, but it's not a way to make a life. Even ten years ago the real mountain men, the trappers, were saying the beaver and other critters were getting over-trapped. Plus, the market isn't there for it anymore. I hear men back East are wearing different hats now, made of some fabric... I don't recall what kind."

"Silk, I think."

Cal gave a little frown. "That doesn't seem very useful to me, but what do I know? Anyway, I learned to trap in the mountains from an old fellow named Jim. When gold was discovered, we both headed down to see what could be seen."

"And what did you see?"

"Well, Jim saw a pack of crazy men and hightailed it back into the hills. I saw opportunity. I met a fellow who'd filed a claim that looked really good, but he got robbed of all his money before he could buy the equipment. So I invested some of my trapping money with him. When I'm in the Virginia City area I go and work the mine with J.B.—that's his name—but mostly, he does it."

"And this works for you both?"

"Yup. I trust him with my life, never mind my mine. Mind my mine... ha! That's a tongue twister.

"But what I really want, is to work my own land. With the mountains nearby, in this beautiful valley."

"It sounds lovely. I grew up on a farm, but I've been—I had been—living in the city since I was seventeen. Don't think I knew how much I missed the land until I got out of the city for more than a couple of days."

"Seventeen? Is that when you went to work in the mill?"

"Yes. My mother passed when I was ten. My father remarried when I was twelve. My stepmother, that's Samuel's mother, she had some grand ideas that meant spending a lot of money. Then my father had an accident and broke both his legs." Cal winced at that. His whole life could be ruined by two broken legs; or at least, all his plans could be derailed.

"If your father had enough money to loan some to Samuel, why did you keep working at the mills?"

Amanda's brow furrowed as her eyes lost the focus, just as

happens when a person delves into their memories. "Their circumstances improved, but... my stepmother was opening the envelopes that I sent and setting the money aside. She told my father she'd saved her pin money, and that was actually where they got some of the money for the loan. Once I learned that, well, I stopped sending them money."

She woke from her memories and looked at Cal again. "I saved what I earned after that. So, when I had the opportunity to come here, how could I resist? After all, I helped fund his store. Or so I thought."

"Considering that you didn't wait to hear from Samuel, I'd say you made the opportunity."

"Well, I did send the letter," she bristled.

"No, you misunderstand," said Cal. "People out here, if they're going to succeed, or even survive, they can't wait for opportunity to come to them. They have to make it happen." He grabbed her hand. "You; you did that. You saw a chance and you grabbed it. You're the kind of person that will survive. You're the kind of woman that can help a man succeed, together. And you're beautiful to boot."

He finished up leaning forward and could hear the passion in his own voice. Here he was, with his fake fiancée, telling her how she was prime wife material. Perfect for him. And from the look on her face, she was warring with modesty and pride deep inside herself.

Cal sat back, taking his hand off hers. He liked Amanda. A lot. Much more than he should. He had no right to sweet-talk her when he was engaged to another woman. He wasn't that kind of man. For a moment though, he wished he could be.

Just then a figure appeared in the doorway, a shadow outlined against those of twilight. Cal's hand slid to his gun. The figure—the man—stepped forward. It was Smitty.

"Smitty!" Amanda whispered on a rush of breath. Cal realized she'd been holding it, scared it was one of Ned's men.

Cal raised a hand in greeting and Smitty walked directly to them. He clapped Cal on the back. "You did it, Cal. You brought her in safely. And from the look of things, Miss Amanda," Smitty said, admiring her clean and neat hair and dress, "you're better off for it."

Amanda gave Smitty a genuine, unreserved smile. She wasn't holding a grudge. Cal felt a bit jealous. She said, "We only had one dangerous encounter with a human animal. How about you?"

Smitty's smile dropped. "What's this? No, we didn't have any more troubles. But you did?" He dropped into the chair beside Cal. "So…?"

"So," said Cal, "turns out Ned Bart is trying to get to Amanda. I'll tell you what we know so far."

"Not now," Smitty cut him off. "There's a group of men unsaddling their horses out at the corral just now. I don't know them, but you don't want to take a chance of them seeing you, Miss Amanda."

Cal and Amanda rose as one. He grabbed her hand and led her back to the staircase.

CHAPTER 15

Amanda sat on the narrow bed of her hotel room. Being the only woman around, at least that she'd seen, meant no one was expecting her to share her room. It was interesting. She'd felt lonely, off and on, for the many months of her journey west, but she'd rarely been truly alone. Oh, sure, she'd had a few moments here and there to run off and tend to her personal needs—but that time hardly lent itself to contemplation.

A few times, on a rest day, she'd wandered off and found a private place to enjoy the scenery that was different from Massachusetts. But in the early days, there'd been a lot of people traveling and not much space unoccupied by anyone else.

By the time they'd traveled far enough West to allow for alone time, she was a little too nervous to venture far from the pack train. Wild animals. Wild Indians. She'd heard stories and that was enough for her.

But even in Lowell, she hadn't had much alone time. She worked on the factory floor with dozens of women. She lived in a boarding house with sixteen others, three of whom had even shared her room.

Now, however, she was on her own. Truly. In a room, with a door. One of the few people she knew for hundreds or thousands of miles around was riding away. The people nearby were few and far between.

And, it seemed, she didn't really want to be. There was an exception to her enjoyment of this strange occurrence. Cal. Calvin; she didn't like being separated from him. It wasn't just that he was aiding her in a time of trouble. It wasn't just that he was terribly handsome. It wasn't just his admirable character.

The night before, at dinner, when he'd talked about what a great homesteading wife she'd be... Well, she'd drunk it in like water to a woman wandering the desert. The idea of building a home and family with a man had never been so appealing. She hadn't felt alone then but on the brink of a partnership. Cal was smart and hardworking, too.

And now, he was riding off to Gallatin City to meet his fiancée. His other fiancée. His real fiancée.

Amanda didn't know what to think about this. What was he going to say to this woman, Delia? What if, upon seeing her, Cal felt a rush of emotion? What if, for whatever reason, he wanted to honor his engagement? And what did that say about her, Amanda, wishing a man would break off his engagement to another woman?

She jumped up off the bed and began pacing the small room. For that is what she did wish... that Cal was free to choose another path... one that involved herself.

There was a knock on the door. She stopped pacing. He'd come back! She smoothed her skirt and rushed to the door. She couldn't help but smile wide. She pulled open the door and halted even before she could say hello.

It wasn't Cal. Her heart sank.

There, at the threshold, stood Pastor Frank with a stranger

behind him. Though it had only been three days since she'd last seen the preacher, it felt like much longer.

"Pastor Frank!" She felt the genuine smile sliding from her face but managed to paste on a polite one. Though they'd traveled in the same pack train for weeks, and she'd found him rather a pest, it wasn't his fault she'd been hoping for Cal and not him.

"Miss Amanda," said Frank, giving Amanda an eager smile. "It is my great pleasure to see you safe and sound."

"Thank you, Pastor Frank." Unlike the last time there was a knock at the door, when it was Cal standing there, she didn't open it wide or give any indication her visitor was welcome into her room.

"I have many things to discuss with you, but first, there is one that is urgent." Frank turned and gestured to the man beside him, who gave her a nod of his head. "This is Miles Carston. He knows your brother."

Miles glanced around the hall, as though someone might overhear them. Amanda stepped into the hallway and spoke quietly. "Do you know where he is? Is he safe?"

Mr. Carston spoke in a low voice, leaning toward her without moving his feet, like a sapling blown by the wind. "I do. He's safe enough, but he's dying. Ain't right for family to be so close at such a time and not get to say their goodbyes."

Amanda's breath caught in her chest. Cal had told her the rumors, that Samuel had been shot, but it was different to hear it so baldly put that he was dying.

"Where is he? Can you bring me to him?"

"Yes, ma'am."

"Ok," she said, thinking aloud. "I need to tell—"

"No, ma'am. I said he's safe enough, but that's because no one knows where he is. It's best no one knows for sure he's nearby."

"I see, yes. Ah," she was flustered, wanting to go to Samuel but recalling Cal's concern that she stayed out of sight. "I guess, we can…" She gestured to the two men.

"No, ma'am," Mr. Carston said again. "I approached the Pastor because I heard he knew you, but I ain't bringing him to no hidey-hole." He glanced around again, as though someone could have snuck into the small hallway without their realizing it. "It's now or never, ma'am. Samuel ain't gonna last too long and if I'm caught with him then neither will I."

Pastor Frank began to worry his hat in his hands. "Say a prayer with him, Miss Amanda. A man shouldn't die alone." Then he added, "And, sometimes… sometimes a man needs to get something off his chest before he goes to face the Lord. You go be there for him."

Amanda hesitated only a moment. There really was no choice. Even if Samuel hadn't been dying, she wanted to talk to him, to figure out what had happened. Surely the rumors of his criminal activities were wrong. Perhaps the actions of another man had been attributed to him, or maybe his own actions had been greatly exaggerated?

He was dying, and she couldn't imagine not reaching out to him, to offer comfort or care if she could. How could she face her stepmother or father, or even herself in the mirror, if she didn't?

"We'll be back…?"

"By supper, if we get a move on."

"Let me get my things. I'll be but a moment."

She stepped into the room and closed the door behind her. She didn't even have a piece of paper or a pen to write a note to Cal. But he wasn't due back until the next day anyway, and she'd be back before then.

CHAPTER 16

Amanda stood at the bedside of Samuel— if you could call it that. He was lying on a bedroll on the floor, a dirty, ratty blanket thrown over him. He was inside a lean-to type shed with canvas draped where the wood was not. The canvas kept the sun away, but not the flies. Samuel lay there, pale under his tanned face, with red spots of color on his cheeks. His fever could be felt before her hand touched his forehead.

"Oh, Samuel."

He was dirty, smelly in a way that combined unwashed man with putrefying wounds. She had thought if she found him, she could help, and they'd find a way out of this mess. But even in her inexperience, she could see death hovering.

Mr. Carston had warned her so, on the ride there. She'd ridden his extra paint pony down the barely-there trail, with several switchbacks and timewasting in shadowy trees to see if they were being followed. She'd had nothing to do but follow and consider Carston's prediction about Samuel. But she'd been sure it couldn't be so bad. Someone who grew up on a

New England farm, at least in his teen years, milking cows and digging rocks out of pastures for crops and walls...? Someone who gave his little stepsister rides on his shoulders, making horse trot sounds...? Someone who'd come back to visit dressed as a dapper store clerk with penny candy for the kids... well, someone like that shouldn't die in a shack across the country, hurt and sick and dirty, and in such pain.

"Why are you here?" Samuel asked in a weak voice. His eyes were dull and half closed.

"I came when your friend said you were hurt."

"No," he paused to cringe as a wave of pain shot through him. "Here. Montana Territory."

Amanda felt a little offended. "I came to help you at the mercantile. What happened to the merc?"

"I told you not to come. Sent... letter."

Amanda's heart sank. She didn't know this unfriendly, sick stranger. He was not the young man she remembered.

"Why... how... I didn't get a letter," she finished lamely, knowing she'd left Lowell before he'd even had a chance to respond.

Samuel was silent, his eyes closed. She wondered how long she should stand there.

"Your father's money," he gasped, struggling. "Bought a claim and mining tools."

"So, there never was a store? But you sent money back to my father."

Samuel continued, seeming to talk to the air because he didn't answer her question or even try to look at her.

"A bust. Gambled. Won a bar. Lost it." He struggled to take a deep breath. "Got in with a gang, y'know... robbing men." He had beads of sweat on his forehead, the effort to talk costing him. "Sent money to pay back, but never enough. Not to repay. Not to escape." His breath grew shallow and he seemed to sink farther into the rags he lay on.

"Why did you bother to write? Why lie?" She couldn't make sense of Samuel's choices. Or the consequences that followed.

"Go," he rasped. "I'll face my maker on my own." His bony hand jerked under the blanket, as though he were trying to wave her away.

Amanda stood there, looking at the shell of the man Samuel had turned into. She felt at a loss. A loss for how to help, and how to connect with him. Even a stranger shouldn't go through this alone, but Samuel felt further away than a stranger and wanted nothing to do with her. Shouldn't he want her to stay with him if only to hold his hand?

The flap behind her lifted and Mr. Carston waved her out.

Well, what about her? She needed more answers before she left. "Samuel, this man Ned; he's looking for me."

Samuel didn't even look at her. "Go. Away. Far."

"They say he wants his gold. That you took it."

"Gold's... gone." He closed his eyes.

"Samuel, this man thinks you'll give him the gold if he gets me first," she was starting to panic. Shouldn't he care, even a little?

"Went looking for a doc, got robbed. Gold's gone." He told her with a rattling breath. "Go."

"I have one more thing to do, Samuel." She knelt at his side, bowed her head and spoke quietly.

"God, I don't know why all this is happening right now. But we know you are here with us. Please help Samuel in his suffering and receive his spirit when it is time."

She looked at Samuel, but he did not open his eyes.

"Amen," she said. After a moment, she stood.

"Goodbye, Samuel." He didn't respond.

Mr. Carston held the flap open as she stepped outside. The sun was gone, hidden behind dark clouds. The temperature had already dropped.

It felt wrong just leaving him there, even despite everything. She imagined how his mother, her stepmother, would be heartbroken to learn of his death. Amanda felt her own loss, but it wasn't for the man particularly, no more than for any other fading and suffering creature. She felt a loss for the memory of affection she'd been carrying these past years, or imagined, and the misplaced pride her father had felt, sending Samuel to Montana Territory with a nest egg to start his own business.

She stepped outside while the friend carried a bundle of rags inside to Samuel. He came back out and began to walk down the path they arrived on. His head was bowed. He said nothing.

She felt a loss of her own dream.

And she felt a loss for her innocence.

Lies, robbery, murder, at least one more with Samuel's impending death. She'd heard the tales, read them in the newspapers and penny dreadfuls, but it hadn't felt real. Tall tales from a storybook. The world was truly more dangerous than she'd realized or wanted to admit to herself.

And even though she'd had a few days to adjust to the idea that the Samuel was not at a mercantile, ready to hire her on as a clerk, she hadn't known how far off the mark she had been. Her dream, based on wishful thinking, had been a fantasy.

"SAMUEL DOESN'T HAVE THE GOLD." IT WAS PART QUESTION, part statement. The man was looking at her, expectant. Waiting.

Amanda came out of her thoughts. Mr. Carsten was leading her back to town and they'd stopped under some cottonwood trees while the clouds poured out small hail.

"What? Yes. He said he was robbed." She found she couldn't care about the gold. It had never existed for her before the previous night. But who could even think about treasure when faced with the decaying body of a man she'd once known as a boy?

"That's not good. Ned will expect you to know where it is." He shook his head and turned to watch the hail bouncing off the ground.

"How should he?" She felt indignant. What right had anyone to involve her in this mess? "It's not my doing," she said.

Mr. Carston brushed a fly off his face. "They're hoping Samuel will have told you on his deathbed."

"No one knows I've gone to him, except Pastor Frank."

"Ned knows where Samuel is. They've been waiting for you to learn Samuel's secret." He paused a moment, and Amanda felt a chill. "Samuel will be dead soon. Ned wants the credit, but he wants the gold more."

Amanda gripped the reins and her whole body tightened, causing the pony to dance around with concern.

"Why did you take me there?"

"Well, last time I went to town I was told it would be beneficial to my health." He turned and looked her straight in the eye. "I've done what I was told to do and now I'm heading out before any new troubles come my way."

"What about——" She was interrupted by a gunshot coming for the direction they'd just left. She spun her pony around. "Samuel! We've got to help him." What could she do? She didn't know, but he was defenseless there.

Mr. Carston reached out and grabbed the pony's bridle before they could start running. She tried to imagine what Cal would do now, but her thoughts were interrupted by the shock of Carston's next words.

"Miss Amanda, that was Samuel finishing things up. No man wants to suffer like that when he knows there's no coming back." He watched her carefully and when he was sure she wasn't going to take off, he let go of the bridle. Then, he tipped his hat as he looked back toward the makeshift camp. He closed his eyes briefly, his lips moving.

Was he a friend? Was he an enemy? Amanda had never had enemies before this trip and didn't know how to categorize a man who performed at the behest—or threat—of a bad guy, but still looked out for a sick man in a way so hard to accept.

Amanda felt scared, angry and relieved all at once. She hadn't known Samuel anymore, didn't want to go into battle for him. But she didn't want him to suffer either. And now, if Mr. Carston was right, he didn't suffer.

Mr. Carston opened his eyes, swung his horse around and headed toward town again. "I'll drop you off in town, and then I'll go back and bury Samuel. After that, you won't see me around here again."

Her pony followed on automatically. The hail had stopped by now, and the sun was pushing through again.

"What... about... a cemetery?" Shouldn't she be able to tell her parents that Samuel was laid to rest properly?

"Bozeman doesn't have a cemetery yet, ma'am."

"Oh."

All Amanda wanted was to get back to her hotel room and hide under the covers until Cal returned. She was surprised how desperately she wanted to be with Cal. Not for protection, but for comfort. Mr. Carston stayed silent until they reached the edge of town. Then he halted the ponies.

"Looks clear," he said. "You can walk in from here."

Despite being so close to the hotel, Amanda felt abandoned. She looked all around them, imaging Ned's men hiding behind every tree and bush. She slid off the pony, handing the reins to Mr. Carston. At least, she realized, the dust had been damped down by the brief hailstorm. The sun was back out and warming up the afternoon, though she felt a chill inside that wasn't about the weather. Amanda looked at Mr. Carston but didn't know what to say.

"Thank you," sounded strange in her ears but she said it anyway.

Mr. Carston tipped his hat to her. "I have two pieces of advice, if you're willing to hear?"

Amanda nodded.

"Be careful who you trust."

She nodded again.

"And don't let on that you don't know how to get to that gold. You'll be signing your own death warrant."

Amanda's hand flew to her heart and she took a step back. With Samuel dead and the gold gone, she'd thought that would be the end of Ned's vendetta. Now Mr. Carston was saying this wasn't the case, that relief couldn't accompany her grief.

Mr. Carston turned his ponies back down the trail. She watched him until the glare of the sun became too much and she faced the town instead. She needed to get back to her room... and hope she didn't run into anyone on the way.

◈

AMANDA HAD SPENT ALL NIGHT IN HER ROOM IN TOWN. She'd gone over and over her meeting with Samuel. She thought back on his visits when she was a child... About how he'd snowed her father and stepmother with his letters home. And in the end, it didn't matter. He was dead and whatever she might have wished was irrelevant.

She was alone now, at least in this part of the world. And, she was disappointed; she'd had such high hopes for a life lived with self-determination. But, she wasn't as scared as she'd expect to be.

Because of Cal.

She had no claim on him, or he on her. If anything, he was claimed by another woman. Despite that, and despite Mr. Carston's admonition, she trusted Cal wouldn't leave her high and dry.

More than that, Amanda believed Cal was growing to care for her. He had shown her his homestead with pride, and she had thought, a little hope. She was so impressed by him. Did he even know that? It wasn't about the land, though it looked to be good land and a good place to live. And it wasn't just his accomplishments, either… but also his character. After seeing the depths to which Samuel had sunk, she realized how much she admired Cal's honest, hard-working self. And he had helped her, a stranger, without qualms. He stood up to bears and to dangerous men dressed as bears!

He'd brought her to a huckleberry patch when she'd said she wanted to try this local berry. He was kind and courteous, strong and tough. He was interesting and handsome…she was veering away from matters of his good character but still it was true. And all of it was attractive.

She didn't blush, yet felt just a little silly dreaming about Cal's good looks. He was commendable, inside and out. Now, she blushed. It seemed she was giving her heart to a man who hadn't asked for it, and who was committed to another woman.

And she had nothing to offer. Less than nothing, because she had an enemy stalking her. Talk about foolish!

She readied herself for Cal's return, pouring water into the washbasin. She washed her face, neck and hands, re-tucked her neckerchief and tidied her hair. And that was all she could do, for now; she needed Cal's help to figure out where to go from there.

She armored herself with as respectable an appearance as she could, so she wouldn't just collapse into his arms. She didn't think they had a future together, but maybe, if she told him how she felt...

There was a knock at the door.

She wished for a mirror but settled for just one last smoothing of her skirt. She opened the door, excited, but with more care after the experience of the day before.

It wasn't Cal.

CHAPTER 17

Cal urged Miss Molly on. His horse was tired, her head bobbing low to the ground. It had been a long ride to Gallatin City the previous day and now they were heading back already. He couldn't wait to see Amanda.

It had been easy to find Delia. Despite being the County Seat, Gallatin City wasn't that big. And every man there was aware of the beautiful woman waiting for Cal. And she was beautiful. He'd been shocked when he found her sitting on the bench on the porch of the hotel. Same brown hair and green eyes. Now, though, she was grown, with luminous skin and a lovely figure. He might have been interested if he hadn't met Amanda first.

As it was, it was strange to greet someone he only remembered as a child, seeing her now as a woman to whom he was engaged. An engagement he wanted to break. He felt like a blackguard.

Cal had ridden in at the end of the afternoon. He'd put up Miss Molly at the stable. There, he was informed about the now locally-famous Miss Cordelia awaiting him. He was told he was a lucky dog.

Upon approaching the hotel he spotted her quickly, sitting quietly in the shade observing the quiet town around her.

"Delia," he said as he stepped onto the porch. He took his hat off.

"Cal?"

They smiled at each other. Delia looked at him appreciatively, and he wondered if she'd have had done the same if he'd looked as he did when he first met Amanda before he'd shaved and cleaned up.

"I am so relieved to see you," Delia said, standing up. She took both of his hands in hers and gave a gentle squeeze. "My, you have changed quite a bit."

Cal laughed. "I could say the same about you."

They stood there, looking at each other for a moment. Memories of home, of growing up, assailed Cal. He didn't miss it often, but right then, the innocence and dreams of childhood were remembered and missed.

He stepped back and gestured to the bench. They needed to talk and the bench was as good a place as any.

"I'm sorry you've been waiting on me. I didn't know until two days ago that you had arrived."

"It's not your fault, Cal. I left home at pretty much the same time your father sent the letter informing you of the plan." Delia gave him a wide-eyed look.

"Still not good at waiting, then, are you?" he asked.

"Not particularly," she said with a grin. "I haven't minded terribly waiting here, for you, because I was on the road—and river—for so long. But I'm looking forward to getting home, wherever that is now, and staying in one place again." Delia gave him a hopeful look.

"About that," said Cal. He felt like a cad. "I know we said we'd see if we suit when you got out here, but it's not going to work."

Delia shrank back from him, gripping her hands in her lap until her knuckles were white. She looked mortified.

"Oh, no!" said Cal. "It's not you. You're lovely. You're beautiful. It's just that, well, I've met another woman. I feel something special for her."

He watched the mortification drop from Delia, but it was immediately followed by a look of defeat. Her shoulders slumped, and her death grip on her hands lessened only slightly.

"I suppose… then, I suppose I will…" She looked around as if a new path would open up for her right then and there. It looked like she was about to cry.

"I won't leave you high and dry, Delia." He shook his head. "I'd like you to go to Virginia City. My business partner J.B. will help you get settled. But, as soon as you leave here, you've got to stop telling people we're engaged." He took a deep breath. "Remember our childhood romps, when I was a knight rescuing the damsel in distress?"

Delia nodded.

"Well, I've found one and fallen for her. But she's in a heap of trouble." Cal paused for a moment to consider Amanda and her *trouble*. He hoped she was safe back at the hotel.

"I'm sorry, Delia. I was honest when I made the plan with you. I figured we would suit. But I hadn't counted on meeting Amanda." He told her about Amanda.

"So you're pretend-engaged to her, too?" Delia raised her eyebrows at him.

"Don't give me that look. You always gave me that look when you didn't like what I'd done."

Delia didn't change her expression, but no longer looked so fragile. She had pulled herself together after the shock.

"Why don't you give me a little time to arrange a room for myself and dinner for us?" he asked. "We have a lot to talk about before I head back to Bozeman in the morning."

"So soon?"

"I'm afraid so."

Cal had left Delia sitting on the bench. In his hotel room, he wrote out a quick note to J.B., asking him to come to Gallatin City to collect Delia and bring her back to Virginia City. He gave it to the front desk to post. He also asked about Samuel Emerson and Ned Bart. He didn't learn anything new.

When he and Delia met again an hour later for dinner in the dining room, he explained all about Amanda, as well as one could explain a woman and her crazy situation. Delia told him of her reasons for moving out West, including her widowing. He enjoyed being reminded of their childhood antics, but as the sky darkened he couldn't help but think of Amanda, alone.

CHAPTER 18

Two scruffy, dusty men stood outside Amanda's door. She didn't recognize them.

"Miss Amanda, we'd be obliged if you'd come with us," said the shorter man. The taller man fingered a gun holstered at his side.

"No, thank you," she said quickly as she tried to close the door. She'd already traveled with two strange men this week and didn't see how going with these two would result in anything better. A booted foot in the door stopped her, and a hand pushed the door open.

"Are you going to make this hard?" the same man spoke. The other gave her a small, unpleasant smile. She wanted to say yes but saw the taller man fingering his gun again. She might get shot by these men right here, or there, wherever *there* was. But if she started screaming, whoever came to help her might get shot, too.

Cal was due back. She cared too much to let him get hurt. Maybe she could meet Ned, tell him Samuel was dead and she had no information about the gold. Maybe she could end this all that same day?

She shook her head, grabbed her hat and stepped out of the room. She pulled the door closed behind her. The shorter man put his hand between her shoulder blades and gave her a shove in the direction of the stairs.

The men put Amanda onto an ancient pack mule. The talker held the reins and led the mule, while the man with the gun rode behind. She'd half expected them to tie her hands. Though she could see no way out of this mess, she was grateful she hadn't been tied.

They had tried to put her on Cal's packhorse; it disturbed her that they'd watched her enough to know she'd traveled with Cal and this was his animal. But she had refused, explaining she wouldn't be party to horse thievery. She could tell they went along because it suited them not to have a scene, but she so disliked the amused glances they shared.

All she knew was that she might not be allowed to come back. No need to take Cal's horse. No need to give him another excuse to chase danger. But it didn't matter. She expected he'd come for her.

She desperately hoped he wouldn't.

She desperately hoped he would.

They followed a trail alongside the creek until they reached a narrow river. It wound through gnarly cottonwoods and red-stemmed willow bushes. At some point, they turned off to a fainter side trail, clearer than a deer track, but not especially. Amanda looked around but the mountains were too far away for an accurate measurement and there was nothing remark-able otherwise. She thought she could probably find her way back, if she was allowed to go back. They hadn't done anything to prevent her from seeing the way. She wasn't sure if this was a good sign, that they didn't intend her harm or a very bad sign. Maybe it wasn't a lair in which Ned would want to remain hidden. Maybe it was a way station. Who knew?

They arrived at a camp under a stand of cottonwood trees.

A small creek muddled through on the way back to the river. From the trampled grass, Amanda could see this was a regularly used camp. There was a fire ring of stones, a fallen log bench, and a tree stump tabletop. Sitting on the bench there and talking to two men was bear man, the big hairy man who'd accosted her in the huckleberry patch.

He rose to his feet, slapping his thighs. "Well, well. We meet again." Amanda stared at him, wondering if he expected some kind of social niceties from her.

He approached her with a smile, but a hard one that didn't make her feel welcome, or even safe.

He reached up to grab her off the horse. He kept his hands on her waist a little too long, her feet barely brushing the ground as he held her. He leaned toward her, speaking low into her ear. "You cost me a nice bounty, little miss. You owe me."

Before she could respond, or even think about how to respond, he slammed her down hard and spun her around. He shoved her toward the two sitting men. One of them, a young man with a pockmarked face, stood and slinked off. The other sat there, appraising her. He looked... like a regular man, a man of the frontier, at least. He had muttonchop whiskers, hair smoothed down, typical miner's town clothes. But he had an intensity. She was reminded of Cal's stories of mountain lions. She whispered to herself, "You'll never see them until it's too late."

CAL UNSADDLED HIS HORSE AT THE STABLE. THOUGH THE town had put itself on the map, it was still more dream than reality. There was no livery stable, offering a fellow to leave your horse with. Cal didn't mind. He liked knowing his animals were cared for the right way.

The right way. He was having dreams of a future with

Amanda, but he wasn't sure it was the right way. He remembered the little farmhouse he grew up in, with cousins down the road and a schoolhouse only a three-mile walk away. He thought of town socials with fiddles and horns, and Sunday morning church. Here, he had land and even a little money. But there was no bank to put the money in. No school. No church, few women. He had a cabin that was little more than a shack.

He planned to tack up newspapers and animal pelts in the fall, to help get through the cold winter in his new home. Was it right to even consider asking Amanda to be with him? He wasn't sure it mattered that the other fiancée was now history. Would Amanda even consider settling down with him while Ned still hunted her?

In Gallatin City, he'd found out nothing new about Samuel or Ned. Nothing that could help Amanda. He imagined what he could say. "Amanda, even though there's another woman recently claiming to be my fiancée, would you marry me—if we can even find a real preacher—and live in my shack and we'll try not to freeze to death this winter?" But with the way he felt, how could he not ask her?

Life in Montana Territory was hard and if she said no because of the house, or the hard work, then he'd know she didn't really belong there... at least, she didn't care enough for him. If she said no because of Ned, well, Cal could work on that.

If her brother and his store had been a respectable choice, he'd have courted her while she worked and lived with Samuel. Or, maybe not. Every Tom, Dick and Harry would be courting her too. Why give them the opportunity to push him out of the picture?

It didn't matter. The situation with her brother was bad news. It was as bad as he'd feared, and it was plain there was no future for Amanda with Samuel.

A selfish part of him was glad. But he didn't want her to accept a proposal from him just because she felt she had no other choice. But then, he thought they'd make out fine together, so maybe a little push wasn't so bad. He realized on this point that he had little pride. He was looking at this in a self-serving manner and cared for Amanda enough that he'd do what he could to make her want to be with him as much as he wanted to be with her. On the other hand, he cared for Amanda enough that it was more important to make her happy than to end up happy himself.

And now, Cal realized he was just standing there, at Miss Molly's side, simply staring into space as all these thoughts bounced around his head and his heart. Cal slapped the flank of his horse to send her off, then turned to walk out of the stable.

One way or another, he'd do his best for Amanda.

AMANDA DIDN'T ANSWER HER DOOR. THE ROOM WAS unlocked and empty. Cal headed back out and found Rumor Rob at the bar, busy soaking his hand in a bucket of water.

"What happened to you?" asked Cal.

"I got stepped on by Buster this morning," said Rob, referencing his mule. He held up his dripping hand. It was bruised and swollen.

"That needs ice," said Cal.

"If only we had some. I'll make do with the cold creek water."

Cal nodded. "Miss Amanda's not in her room."

"The first time she left—" said Rob.

"First time?" Cal interrupted.

"Yes. She left with Mr. Carston. He was slinking a bit, but you can't go unnoticed here."

"Who is Carston?"

"He's a shady fellow, hanging on the outskirts of trouble." Rob saw Cal's alarm. "Not so bad as Ned Bart and his crew. I'm talking card cheat, some thievery. But he was friendly with Samuel, I'd heard. That Pastor Frank brought him in and up to Miss Amanda's room."

Cal wondered why she'd go off with a man she just met. But then, she'd gone off with him...

"They were gone about five hours, yesterday. Then today, two fellows who work for Ned showed up. Miss Amanda left with them not long after. Down the crick." He pointed north.

Cal felt anger and panic and worry—and a whole slew of emotions rising up inside him. While he'd been daydreaming, his love was entering the den of the lion.

Rob continued, "Ned thinks no one knows, but he's got a camp off the Gallatin, about five miles west. Beans to butter, that's where they're headed."

Cal wanted to shake Rob, shout, "Why did you let her go?" but all he said was, "Thanks, Rob."

Cal took two steps toward the door when Smitty and Pastor Frank walked in. Smitty walked right up to Cal and poked him in the chest.

"Where have you been? Your Amanda's gone and left with Ned Bart's men. Are we going to go get her?"

Rob said, "Take a moment, Cal, to get collected and you can have even more company. Some other townsfolk have had about enough of Ned and this is as good a reason as any to say enough is enough." He paused only a moment. "I can see you wish I'd kept her from leaving with them, but, well, y'know... I was alone and with this hand, I'd have been more of a danger to Miss Amanda than a help."

Cal didn't want to wait beyond the time it took him to saddle up, check his ammunition and prime his gun, but Smitty grabbed his shirt as he tried to pass.

"Getting yourself killed won't help Miss Amanda. Like Rob said, take a moment."

Cal felt the tide of fear and anger rising inside of him.

"I have an idea," said Pastor Frank, hesitatingly. "I can go to this Ned Bart fellow and ask him to let Amanda go."

"Why would he listen to you?" Cal snarled.

"Because I'm a man of God," said Pastor Frank, his hesitation fading in his conviction of God's grace. He squared his shoulders. "I know there's risk. I want to do this, for Amanda."

Cal felt an unusual emotion swirling inside him. It was possessiveness. He didn't want Pastor Frank to rescue Amanda. He wanted to rescue her himself. She was his.

Cal took a step forward, the sound of his boots echoing on the wood floor. He looked at Pastor Frank. Frank stood his ground but leaned back ever so slightly at Cal's menace. He looked like he might start trembling at any moment.

"I... I mean, I don't think he'll just hand her over! I'll delay him a bit... while you fellows get a posse together," said Pastor Frank, his voice trailing off.

Cal still didn't like it. He didn't want to stall. He wanted to tear after Amanda, screaming a warrior's call, weapons poised. He wanted to rescue her now. He wanted to know she was safe.

He wanted what was best for Amanda.

Cal exhaled his pent-up frustrations and hotheaded ideas, giving a curt nod.

Smitty said, "Good. I'll go alert Richard and Scamp."

Rumor Rob said, "I'll go see if Sheriff Mendenhall is back in town and get anyone else I can find."

Cal said, "After you tell Pastor Frank where to find Ned's camp."

"Right," said Pastor Frank with a look of surprise. "I need to know that."

Cal wondered if this naïve man could really help Amanda. Well, one thing was for sure: they would soon find out.

"I'll go saddle the horses," said Cal, "starting with yours, Pastor Frank." Anything to feel like he was making progress toward Amanda. "You have one hour. We're leaving here in one hour to follow, whether it's just me and Miss Molly, or the whole town." He wasn't going to leave Amanda there unprotected a moment longer than necessary.

CHAPTER 19

Amanda wished she had screamed her head off when those two men had shown up at her hotel room. She should have screamed loud and long. Because, as scary as it was to imagine what bad things could happen, she was pretty sure it paled into insignificance compared to what Ned would do to her if she didn't produce a treasure soon.

How foolish of her to not demand a solution from Samuel!

He'd siphoned off Ned's stolen money and then gone and shot Ned's cousin. It was Samuel's fault she was in this mess.

Okay, being honest with herself, maybe that wasn't the whole truth; she'd come out West without proper planning. She didn't receive any kind of sign from Samuel that she was wanted, or even that she might stay with him short term, even if she wasn't wanted. And now, she'd foolishly agreed to meet Ned, or at least not been dragged out of her hotel room kicking and screaming.

She sat on the ground at the base of the cottonwood tree. Its huge branches and leaf canopy gave her a pleasant shade from the strong sun bearing down on the valley. Ned hadn't even bothered to tie her hands. She thought about their introduction. The big bear man—Ned called him Ollie—had shoved her to sit beside Ned on the downed log.

"You are far too pretty to be the sister of Big Em."

It gave her chills just to be under observation by Ned, with his golden eyes.

"He was my half-brother."

"Was?"

"I—I heard you shot him." Shoot, she didn't know if it was better if Ned thought Samuel was alive or dead.

"Think he'll come out of hiding if he hears I have you?"

"No. We are not close."

"But you came out here to work with him," Ned said, pulling Amanda's own letter from his vest pocket; the letter she'd written to Samuel, telling him she was coming West to work with him. "He must have a soft spot for you if he agreed to that."

"I didn't... I didn't wait for his response..." she said, "because I wasn't sure he would agree." It felt wrong to be conversing with this criminal, but she couldn't see how it would help her to do otherwise.

"You've got gumption!" Ned threw back his head and laughed. Then, in an instant, the humor dropped from his face and he swiveled his piercing eyes back to hers. "But, it doesn't help me. I want my money. I want my respect."

His low tone sent chills up her back.

"I don't have your money."

"No. What you don't have is the proper respect for me." He leaned in close. "Because you seem to think you can lie to me. You seem to think you can wriggle your way out of this situation. But you can't." His eyes drilled into hers.

She tried to look away but he grabbed her chin and forced her face to confront his. "Listen, little missy. I know you went to see Samuel. I know he's dead. I know your boyfriend left for Gallatin City. I know you don't have anyone."

He paused and let that sink in, and it sank, all the way to the pit of her stomach. She had never been so frightened.

"The only thing you can do is decide whether you will tell me where my gold is. Once I have it, I will kill you quickly." His hot breath washed over her face and she saw a dimming at the edge of her vision. "Or you can make me draw out your death. Real slow and tortuous, until you tell me where the gold is anyway."

Don't pass out, Amanda told herself.

A distant part of her watched her own self and was disappointed, wishing she had more backbone and didn't bow to this man so quickly, so easily.

A whistle broke the moment. Ned released her and jerked back quickly, scanning the edges of the camp. He pulled his gun and stood up, close beside Amanda, holding her in her seat on the tree stump with his hand pushing down on her shoulder. She took deep breaths, trying to get her head clear. Several more whistles called out.

"What?" she whispered, not daring to say more.

"Someone is coming. For you. You are not so alone, after all," he said in a low tone.

Amanda knew only one person would come for her.

As she had hoped and feared. Cal.

"Maybe now you'd like to tell me where the gold is. Because if you don't,"—his fingers dug into her shoulder—"your friend will die right now. And you'll earn a long, drawn-out death for yourself." The fingers released, but the pressure did not. "And you'll still tell me where my money is first."

Amanda heard a rumble of thunder. In the distance, to the west, a line of dark grey storm clouds was blowing in. She saw a flash of lightning far off in the distance.

She was more scared of the man behind her than even the lightning headed her way. Far more scared.

"I... I don't... I don't know..."

Ned growled. His hand left Amanda's shoulder to dig into her hair. He yanked her forward off the log shoving her to her hands and knees on the ground. She remained there, staring at the dirt in front of her face, bracing for what came next.

A pair of feet shuffled up to them. Not Cal. She felt a welling of gratefulness that Cal was safe. But it was also a welling of despair, for he'd been her last hope.

She looked up slowly, still waiting for another bout of violence from Ned Bart.

Pastor Frank! What?

He stood with his feet braced slightly, as though poised for battle, but ruined the effect by once again worrying his hat in his hands. He looked at her as he stood squinting in the sunlight, just outside the shade that covered Amanda and Ned.

"Miss Aman—Miss Amanda," he stuttered, "I—I'm here to help you." He turned his squint to Ned Bart. "I de—demand you h—hand her over."

Oh, dear God, thought Amanda. *He is a dead man. Oh, poor man.*

She grappled for anything to stave off the inevitable reaction of Ned Bart. And then, Pastor Frank dissolved into laughter.

Ned Bart shoved his gun into its holster. He stepped forward and grabbed Pastor Frank in a bear hug. The two men slapped each other on their backs, laughing. When they pulled apart, Pastor Frank was a new man. He didn't worry his hat. His shoulders lost some hunch. He stood a little taller with his hands braced on his hips. His face was... Amanda struggled to decipher it. Confident? Satisfied?

"Cousin!" said Ned. They hugged again.

"Ned! It's been too long, boy!"

"Pastor Frank?" Amanda was still on the ground, but she'd sat back on her heels, watching the pastor as though through a pane of wavy glass. He was not himself. Or, he was not the self she had thought he was.

His demeanor changed again, back to the man she had known these past few weeks. He held out his hand to help her rise. She took it, knowing that behind that obsequious, smiling face was a snake, but mesmerized by him anyway. She slid her hand out of his and backed up until the backs of her legs pressed against the log.

He gave her a slight bow. "I'm not actually a pastor, you know," he mock-whispered in his kind Pastor-voice.

Lightning quick, Frank changed again. He grinned at Ned and gave a deep, theatrical bow. Ned began to clap. "She never suspected, I see," he said with a nod of approval.

"None of them suspected," Frank said, hooking his thumbs into his pants pockets. The two men turned to look at Amanda, expectant.

"Who are you?" she said. Part of her didn't care. She just wanted to disappear from this nightmare. But part of her did want to know; she wanted to know why this was happening.

"Jedidiah Frank, at your service," said the man she'd thought was Pastor Frank. It was almost hard to look at him, like seeing someone you'd heard so much about that you thought you knew them, but where the real person didn't match the one in your head. She looked between the two men. There was a faint resemblance.

"Why?" she asked.

"That cousin of Ned's that Big Em killed? That was my brother," said Jedidiah. He leaned in, his eyes steely. "My brother. Get me?"

"That had nothing to do with me," she cried. Death and violence, lies and traps were swirling about her. She wanted to escape it all.

Ned raised his hand to stop Amanda from continuing. To stop her from becoming hysterical, she suspected.

"It has everything to do with you. I can't have folks thinking me and mine can be killed without sufferin' the consequences. You—" he pointed his finger at her, "are a consequence."

Jedidiah interrupted Ned. "Speaking of consequences, there's a posse of them headed this way. But I think I can stop them with a little help from our girl here."

His possessive gaze made Amanda feel sick in her stomach. "Your special friend Cal is leading the charge. Tell me what to say to him to make him turn around."

The sick feeling in Amanda's stomach became a leaden weight that threatened to topple her. If she helped Pastor Frank—no, Jedidiah Frank—she was lost. She had no treasure. Her chances of escaping this situation unharmed were slim, but without the gold, Ned would not let her survive.

A loud crash of thunder boomed around them, and a bright streak of lightning lit up the sky. Even Ned took a step back at the powerful weather swirling about them.

Amanda thought about Cal, and how much she cared for and admired him. How much she loved him. No use trying to fool herself now. She didn't want to put him in harm's way. But one of the reasons she admired him was that she knew he wouldn't be swayed by any words passed on by another person, such as the man Cal knew as Pastor Frank. Cal would make sure Amanda was safe, even if she didn't want him to.

The rain plastered her hair to her head and washed away the tears that leaked out.

"Do you want me to meet Cal, and tell him to go away?"

The two men laughed. But Ned's laugh turned ugly. He grabbed Amanda's arm tightly and shoved his face into hers. "No, you're not going to meet him and bat your eyelashes at him. Think you can escape? You can't," he hissed.

Chills ran through Amanda. There was a kind of madness in Ned's eyes. Carefully, slowly, she said, "I could... I could send a message through Pastor Frank. I think Cal has grown to care for me. I think I can... dissuade him." Her heart sank at the cruel message she needed to send to Cal, and at how she needed to hurt him. Even knowing she'd try to send a secret message that would tell Cal the truth, she wasn't sure he'd receive it if he believed the hurtful one.

Ned stepped back. His face untwisted. In the voice and demeanor of a man used to being in charge, he said, "Tell him," and gestured to the faux pastor. Then he walked away.

Jedidiah Frank faced Amanda. "This better be good. Try to trick me, and I'll have a knife ready for Cal." He said it so matter-of-factly, Amanda wondered if madness ran in their family.

She took a deep breath.

"Tell Cal," she said, "I can't be involved with a man who already has a fiancée."

"Whoa!" Jedidiah grinned. "Now that's unexpected."

"Tell him," and at this, Amanda's heart began to break, "that I've found my own path, and it doesn't include him."

"He's going to argue with me."

"I know. That's when you tell him he must believe me... just as..." she pretended to search for a response. "Just as Jim believed in the gold of Alder Gulch. Tell him if we meet again, under the right circumstances—if lightning strikes twice—perhaps we'll have a future together."

As if on cue, another bolt of lightning lit the sky, this time farther east. The eye of the storm was passing them by.

Frank eyed Amanda, and she knew he was trying to judge whether the message would work. She explained.

"Cal learned trapping from Jim, but when gold was struck, they came down to the valley together. Cal told me the story and—he'll know I told you." She hesitated but figured a dose of truth couldn't hurt now. "I really can't be sure if he'll believe you, but it's the best I can think of. Please, turn him away. Please, don't hurt him." Her voice turned to a whisper.

Jedidiah stepped closer to Amanda, leaning in. "I'll do what I can," he whispered, "for you, Miss Amanda. Being a man of God, and all." He smirked.

A shudder ran through Amanda. She leaned away. Jedidiah put a finger onto her shoulder, on the fabric wet from the rain. He began to draw it down her arm. Amanda stepped away and twisted to face him. She gripped her hands together in front of her.

"How did you find me? In Laramie? And how did you tell Ned where to find us?" She almost sighed with relief when she saw Jedidiah's eyes light up, ready to tell his side of the story. He grinned.

"Ah, now that's a story of luck and cunning. Ned had your letter to Big Em in hand. He wrote to me, telling me about your brother, and my brother's murder, and about how you would likely travel through Fort Laramie. I became Pastor Frank and waited for you. Simple as that. It was dumb luck you wanted to leave your situation, and that Smitty was ready to take the Bozeman Trail at just the right time. As soon as I met you, I sent a letter to Ned and told him my plan. He had just enough time to send some men out to ambush the mule train." He lost his grin. "It would have worked if Cal hadn't come along."

That mention of Cal's name reminded them both that Jedidiah had to go to intercept Cal. Apparently, Ned remembered too, because bear man Ollie strode up, saying, "Ned says you better get going. Now."

He only glanced at Jedidiah but stood there menacing at Amanda. The rain had let up, and the heat of the day was returning. Ollie's animal skins lightly steamed and a rank smell surrounded him. It made Amanda want to gag.

She sat back on the log, wrapping her arms around her

waist. Ollie took up sentry near her. Jedidiah walked back out of camp. Ned was conferring with his other men. Here she was, surrounded, trapped, and wondering if Cal would understand her message. It wasn't very good. It's not as though she'd had time to plan it.

Would Jedidiah end up killing Cal? Or would Cal try to rescue her, and then Ned might kill him instead? She took a gasping breath, willing herself to stay calm. This wasn't over yet. As long as her heart was beating, there was a chance she could survive.

But without Cal, she wasn't sure she wanted to.

CHAPTER 20

Cal stood over a patch of mud in the road outside Rumor Rob's hotel. On it was drawn a crude map. Bozeman, the creek, the East Gallatin River, a few other landmarks, and most importantly, Ned Bart's supposed camp. The storm had passed through quickly, dropping enough rain to turn the dirt road into a literal drawing board.

He was surrounded by Rob, Smitty and Dick, Sheriff Mendenhall, and four other men who'd been in town that afternoon and were willing to form a posse. It was killing him to leave Amanda out there, at the mercy of Ned Bart and his men. But he recognized what the men had said was true; getting himself killed wouldn't help Amanda.

A whistle pierced the air. It was Scamp; they'd set him on watch duty. That single, long whistle meant Pastor Frank was returning to town. A moment later, Scamp ran up to the men. He had that eager excitement that came only with youth, with not understanding the consequences of real-life adventures.

"It's Pastor Frank coming!"

Cal's throat seized and he couldn't speak.

Smitty spoke for him. "With Miss Amanda?"

"No, sir. He's alone."

Pastor Frank appeared on the road, turning the corner from the north. Cal studied the pastor's appearance. He hadn't been roughed up but he didn't look happy. He didn't look completely dejected, either. He wasn't, Cal thought with relief, hauling a body. But he did look concerned. Pastor Frank had seemed interested in Amanda in a personal sense; surely, he'd look grieved if he knew she had been injured... or killed.

Pastor Frank halted his horse just outside the circle of men. Scamp stood at the horse's head, ready to tie it to the hitching post when the rider dismounted. Frank slid off the horse and landed with a wobble. He held onto the saddle a brief moment, catching his balance. Cal couldn't stand the delay.

"Well?" he barked.

Frank flinched. He turned to face the men. The pastor didn't quite meet Cal's eyes. He took his hat off and began to worry it in his hands.

"I saw her. She was unharmed."

Relief flooded Cal. He actually stumbled back a step.

"Spit it out," said Smitty.

Pastor Frank squared his shoulders. "I saw Miss Amanda. She is with Ned Bart. They—" He hesitated. "They worked out a deal. Miss Amanda is going to bring him to the gold that Big Em stole, and in return, Bart will let her live."

Of all the things Cal had imagined hearing, this was not it. Amanda had made a deal with Ned Bart? She knew where to find the missing gold? He felt a mixture of relief and confusion. Disbelief washed over him next.

It must have shown on his face because Pastor Frank rushed to add more to the story. "She got the location from Big Em yesterday. He's dead, by the way."

"God rest his soul," rolled quietly through the group of men.

Frank continued speaking.

"Miss Amanda told Ned there's more gold than from that one robbery. That's what Big Em said, anyhow. And Miss Amanda promised it all to Ned, except for enough to get her started in Virginia City. A *nest egg*, she called it. Ned's going to deliver her to Virginia City, after. And then, Miss Amanda can make her own way in life…"

Frank sighed and hung his head slightly as if disappointed not to have better news.

Cal watched as the tension dropped from the men around him, even as it rose inside himself. This didn't feel right. Would Amanda just abandon all her belongings? Abandon Cal?

"You don't believe this, do you?" Cal looked around at all the men. "She spoke under duress. Ned Bart's got her and she said what he told her to say."

The other men all turned to the Sheriff. "I'm inclined to agree with Cal. I don't think we can trust what Pastor Frank has told us. No offense, Pastor."

Pastor Frank shook his head. He looked a little embarrassed. "There's more. She said, because she knew Cal might not believe her, to tell him this." He looked up, as though trying to find her exact words written in the sky. "She said to tell Cal he could believe me like Jim believed in the gold of Alder Gulch. She said you'd understand this." Pastor Frank looked relieved to have remembered and delivered the message.

The other men all turned to look at Cal, to assess the value of it. There was pity on the face of some of them, who thought Cal was sweet on a girl now taking up with Ned Bart.

Cal felt a red anger wash over him. This was a secret message. The old trapper Jim had retreated into the mountains when he saw the craziness the discovery of gold had created in the men mining in Alder Gulch. He didn't believe in the gold at all. And now Cal had his truth: he shouldn't believe the message. Or the messenger.

"Was there anything else?"

"She said," Pastor Frank recited, "To tell you that if you and Miss Amanda met again under the right circumstances—if lightning were to strike twice—perhaps you'd have a future together." He said it as if he didn't believe it. A brush-off.

Cal stood there, taking deep breaths, all the men looking at him from under the brims of their hats. He knew now; he knew exactly what she was telling him. She was going to lead Ned Bart to the twice-lightning struck tree on his property. If Cal should set out to rescue Amanda, then he should head there.

He felt as though a balloon was inflating inside of him. It was filled with such a multitude of conflicting emotions. Relief, that Amanda was alive and communicating with him. Joy, that she hoped for a future with him. Fear, that he wouldn't succeed in rescuing her. And then last of all came anger. Red hot, seething and raging anger because Pastor Frank was not to be trusted. He wondered if the Pastor had been playing them this whole time, or if Ned Bart had bought him off just now?

But, under the circumstances, it didn't matter.

Cal drew his gun and pointed it at Pastor Frank. A collective gasp. The other men all stepped back.

"Sheriff," Cal said, "You're going to need to lock this man up."

Murmurs came from the other men, but before anyone could formulate a question, Cal continued, "And then we need to go rescue my Amanda."

CHAPTER 21

Amanda sat on her borrowed horse again and tried to lead Ned and his men to Cal's homestead. She felt terrible bringing these appalling men to Cal's homestead, but she just didn't want to die. She could only keep trying to find a way out of this mess. She hoped that Cal had understood her clues and knew where she was going, that he wanted to rescue her.

But what could Cal do? Amanda remembered the attack on the pack train, and how he'd killed off or scared off the attackers. But even if he received the message from Jedidiah Frank, understood it and wanted to act on it, even if he and Jedidiah didn't tangle then and there, Cal might not have enough time to get to Amanda. She took the smallest comfort in the hope that Ned Bart would leave her body by the tree, where Cal would find it. And she hoped he would find it in him to write to her father.

Her thoughts were interrupted by that normal-sounding voice that belied Ned's dangerous character. "Miss Amanda, are you trying to figure how not to take me to the gold?"

"No, no. I haven't been there. I only know what Samuel

told me. So, I don't know exactly where I'm going." That last was true. She had only been there once and now she was approaching from a different direction. She feared she'd arrive before Cal had a chance to get there and set a trap; at least, she hoped he would get there and set a trap. But, in fact, she was confused by the landscape all the false trails and wrong turns she had inadvertently taken were working to her advantage.

Ned looked at her with his hard eyes, probing her veracity.

"But, I think we're almost there. This way." She clucked her horse forward. Up ahead, there was a stand of cottonwood trees. Lightning had split one tree and she recognized it. This was it. It was the twice-struck tree. Without moving her head, she looked out from under her lashes, looking for a sign Cal was near.

CAL CROUCHED ALONG THE BANK OF THE CREEK, PEEKING through a stand of sagebrush. Sheriff Mendenhall was behind a cottonwood tree. Smitty, Dick and the other four men were placed around the stand of trees, behind willow bushes, along the creek bed, and by some real thick grass. They'd had to leave their horses tied up farther up creek. It was not an ideal place for an ambush, not with the lack of trees and rocks to hide behind. On the other hand, Ned and his men wouldn't have anything to hide behind, either.

Except—of course—they had Amanda.

They'd left Pastor Frank locked up in town, with Scamp to watch over him. Cal knew from Amanda's message that Frank was not to be trusted, but the Sheriff had still apologized as he'd locked the good pastor up. Cal only hoped that Frank hadn't been supposed to meet back up with Ned Bart; that could really tip their hand.

Cal strained to hear their approach, praying Amanda was still safe. He wished she knew he was a free man. He wished he'd already declared his love and proposed to her. If they were going to die—and there was a chance they both could—then he wanted her to know how he felt.

Cal felt an overwhelming mixture of love and fear rising up inside his chest. How could he both find Amanda and lose her within days? He took a deep breath and closed his eyes, focusing on the sounds he could hear around him: the grass rustling under a light breeze; the burbling creek; and the call of a meadowlark.

He opened his eyes as he heard something else. It was the alarm call of a crow. The noisy bird was alerting his feathered friends to the approach of strangers.

No, he told himself, he would not lose her. Not today. Not ever.

After a long minute or two, he heard the clop of a hoof on a rock and his heart jumped as Amanda rode into the clearing. She sat stiffly, her eyes scanning around. He saw when she caught a glimpse of movement in the thick grass. Her eyes kept scanning, though she very carefully didn't move her head. She was, no doubt, afraid of giving away a rescue. Giving away Cal's presence.

She turned her horse, casually, as if she simply was disinclined to dismount. However, she was carefully aimed toward the other gentle trail that would lead her into the willow thickets and on to the creek.

Ned rode up behind her, with two more men and their horses crowding the clearing. One of them was Ollie Lindquist, still dressed in his bearskins. Cal wished he knew if there were more men holding back. At least the Sheriff should get a good look at any men bringing up the rear.

Amanda made a show of looking around before she pointed to the base of the tree. "There," she said. "He said he buried it under this tree."

"My gold had better be there," said Ned.

Amanda's face grew anxious and Cal could only imagine the knots in her stomach. "I only know what Samuel told me."

Ned swung off his horse, hopping down with the lithe movements of a man at one with his horse and with the world around him. He pushed aside the plants, looking for any sign of a piece of earth that had been dug up at some previous point.

As he poked at the roots with his booted foot, Amanda charged forward on her horse. She unknowingly ran straight at Cal. He leaned left as the horse leaned right. Behind her, he saw Ned swinging around, gun in hand and aiming at Amanda's back. Cal ducked under the horse's hooves even as he shot at Ned. Ned flinched at the impact, and then spun around as he was shot from Smitty's direction. The unofficial deputies stood up, guns cocked and aimed, at Ned's remaining men. It had happened so fast one of them never even got a shot off. Ollie Lindquist had fired toward the Sheriff in the trees, but it clearly hadn't hit him, as he was racing toward them.

There was an odd ringing in the air, the sound that comes when several gunshots go off at close range, and the echo of Amanda's horse's hooves as she raced away. The smell of gunpowder and smoke hung thick in the air. Cal held his second pistol, watching Ned and his men for any moves against Cal's group. Ned didn't move. The other two men put up their hands.

Cal rose from his crouch and walked toward Ned with treading-on-eggshell steps as he anticipated a possible jump from Ned. But Ned didn't move. Cal toed him and then rolled him over.

"Is he dead?"

Amanda had come back. She sat on her horse, her face pale under flaming patches of fear and stress on her cheeks.

Cal wasn't ready to smile yet, even though he was so very glad Amanda was unhurt. "You should have stayed away until

I gave you the all clear." She really was getting a greenhorn's introduction to the Wild West.

She looked straight into his eyes. "I couldn't stay away, not if you might be hurt, or needed help, whatever little help I could offer." Her eyes filled with tears. "I couldn't leave you."

Cal's heart filled up his chest.

CHAPTER 22

Cal hammered a stake into the ground. Amanda pulled a piece a twine tight to it and tied it off. They had created a large rectangle in the meadow.

"I'm glad you agreed to come back here," Cal said, waving his arm to encompass his homestead. "I was concerned it might be too soon for you."

They'd gone back into town with the Sheriff, the day before, after the shootout. Cal had helped pack the bodies onto a horse, while Amanda had tended to the wounds of the men of the posse; they were just scrapes. Once in town, Cal had gone with two other men to help dig a grave, while Amanda explained to the Sheriff what had led up to the shootout. She had to tell him about the attack on the pack train, the bear man, and Samuel and the gunshot she'd heard. It was hard to believe all this had taken place in just the past few days.

By the time she'd finished, she was exhausted. The Sheriff escorted her back to the hotel. She waved away an offer of a meal from Rumor Rob and headed straight upstairs. She'd intended to wait up for Cal, but within minutes she'd fallen asleep on top of her bed, still fully dressed.

In the morning, Cal was waiting for her. He'd asked her to ride with him back to his homestead. "This is where the front door will be, and eventually, a porch. We'll have a window in each wall." He pointed to the northeast corner. "We'll put the cook-stove over there."

"We?"

Cal stepped up right in front of Amanda. He took both of her hands in his. "You and me. If you'll have me."

Her heart started pounding. Her breath caught. "What about…?"

"Delia? Told her I couldn't marry her. I still want to help her, but I can't marry her. I want to marry you." He tugged her closer, so she felt they were standing in the same place, breathing the same air. "Amanda, will you marry me?"

Her heart swelled as she tightened her fingers around his. "Yes, Cal." Anything else she had to say was lost when he leaned in, slowly, to press his lips against her own.

His lips were warm and sweet, and with the warmth of the sun on her back and the gentle buzzing of insects in the meadow and birds chirping in the distance, she felt as if she was floating through Heaven, connected to the earth only through her lips pressed up against Cal's.

Suddenly, she was truly flying. Cal lifted her into the air and spun her around. He gave a great, "Yahoo!" She threw her arms around his neck and laughed, the joy spilling out of her.

Cal placed Amanda back on the ground but pulled her in close when she put her hand on his arm. He turned back to the stake and twine rectangle that was marked out beside them. "Can you live here, Amanda? We can move the house if you don't like the location."

She felt she could live in a tent for the rest of her days, as long as she was with Cal. "It's perfect," she said. "As long as I'm with you."

They stepped over the twine to stand inside their home-to-be. "Could you make shelves here?" she asked, pointing to the north wall.

"Yes," Cal said, "and we'll have a wall here to divide the house into a living area and a sleeping area."

"Oh, Cal. It'll be perfect." She smiled at him. "I can't stop saying that."

Cal turned a little nervous. "I can't offer you a big house, yet, and especially not a life of ease."

"I'm not expecting a life of ease."

"Well, I have one project which should help a little." He stepped over the twine, heading toward the northwest, away from the house and creek. He stopped about thirty feet away. "I can't offer you all the amenities you're used to from the city, but I can offer you this. First thing I'll build is your own... private... outhouse."

Amanda laughed. She already had a list of reasons why she loved him, but here was one more.

EPILOGUE

Amanda heard the thwack of an ax hitting on wood, carrying across the crisp, bright air. Cal was working non-stop to finish trimming each log in preparation of the house-raising party they were having in two days' time. It seemed after the long winter that everyone around was excited at a reason to get together. Amanda, in turn, was excited to have their neighbors—however distant—come to the homestead.

She looked up. Though the mountains were still snow-covered, the ground in the valley was down to bare patches of snow. She walked along, hoping to find signs of vegetation she might recognize, like wild asparagus, but it was a little too early in the season. She had found shooting stars and glacier lilies, beautiful wildflowers that glistened like precious jewels. She crouched down to admire the little flowers.

Another thwack reached her ears.

She needed to get back to the dugout cabin to start baking pies. She needed to get back to Cal.

Amanda picked up her pace. Even after getting married last fall, even after an entire, long, winter cooped up together, she still thrilled at seeing Cal after every small break. She kicked up her skirts as she dashed down the hill. After what felt like forever, she saw Cal, shirt off, swinging his ax into a giant log. He had spent much of the winter dragging trees he'd felled in the fall, using the snow to help make it easier on the horses. When the snow hadn't been too deep, that was.

Cal stopped when he saw Amanda. He put the ax down and they ran into each other's arms. He picked her up and gave her a spin around, before sliding her to the ground and placing a kiss on her lips.

"Hello, dear wife."

"Hello, dear husband."

They stood for a moment in giddy silence. Would this feeling ever end? *I hope not*, Amanda thought.

She looked toward the stone foundation Cal had laid, outlining the dimensions of their house to come. Stone by stone he had stacked them, trying to place each one perfectly. On the dark, cold winter evenings they'd cuddled by the fire, talking about the house they were building. Cal said he wanted a house that didn't have meadow mice occasionally dropping from a sod roof. Amanda would say she looked forward to a wooden floor again, instead of the dirt floor they'd been living with. With Ned Bart dead and the fake Pastor Frank in jail they felt free to dream of their future together.

"A fellow on his way out of town stopped by," said Cal, his arms still wrapped around Amanda. "He had been in Virginia City a few months back. Seems J.B.'s doing well with the mine." He gave her a squeeze. "Our mine. We might need to make a trip there soon."

"Any news about Delia?" Amanda asked.

"He didn't know of any. But he did have a letter for you." Cal stepped away from Amanda and toward the stones. He took an envelope that was sitting on his shirt and brought it back to her. "It's from your father."

Amanda opened it and quickly scanned it. She looked up at Cal. "They received my letter about Samuel. I wondered if my letter would make it last fall." She read a little more. "They're grieving."

"Do you feel you made the right decision?" asked Cal.

"Yes. They don't need to know about Samuel's bad choices, or the details of how he died. It won't hurt them to think well of him still."

She folded the letter back up and tucked it into her apron pocket. "I'll read the rest later. Right now," she said, lowering her voice to a whisper so that Cal had to lean into hear her, "I want to know what's in that basket sitting over there."

The basket sitting on the corner stone was one she'd never seen before. Cal gave her a mischievous grin. He stepped away and toward the stones. He lifted up the basket and brought it over. Suddenly it lurched in his hand and gave a little whimper.

"What—?" she asked as she lifted the lid.

A little brown puppy peeked out at her. He was the color of milky coffee, with a patch of white encircling one eye. He began to scrabble, sensing this was his moment to escape the basket. Amanda reached in. She brought the puppy to her chest. He rested his head, perhaps listening to her heartbeat.

"He's beautiful," she whispered. "He, right?"

"Yes, he," said Cal.

They stood for a moment, watching the puppy trying to wriggle his way deeper into Amanda's arms as if it was possible.

She looked up at Cal, eyebrows raised in question.

"That fellow dropped off more than your letter. Last trip to town I heard a litter had been born. I had Rumor Rob tell them that we wanted one of the pups. This little one is not much use now, but he will be. I don't like leaving you all alone here. When I'm checking my traps or off hunting I want to know you have a little bit of protection."

Amanda glowed. Cal was always thinking of her. Always trying to take care of her and make her life a little better.

"So wonderful," she said.

"He's pretty cute," Cal agreed.

"He is," said Amanda. "But I meant you. You are so wonderful, Cal. I'm so lucky to have you." She felt her eyes tear up from the welling emotions inside her.

Cal stepped up, wrapping Amanda in his arms again, with the puppy wiggling between them.

"No," he said, with intent in his eyes. "I'm the one who is so lucky to have you."

They smiled into each other's eyes.

It felt like the puppy, their new house, the mountains and the sun were all smiling with them.

❦

THANK YOU SO MUCH FOR READING! IF YOU ENJOYED THIS book, please take a moment to leave a review.

ABOUT THE AUTHOR

I live in Bozeman, MT, with my husband and three children. I've lived in Canada, Japan, and parts of the U.S., but my heart is in Montana.

I was introduced to romances as a a teenager. One of my fondest memories is sitting on the beach on Cape Cod reading romances that had all the naughty parts blacked out with a thick black marker.

f